The Portal

—— BOOK 1 ——

THE IMAGER CHRONICLES

Formerly titled *Journeys to Fayrah*

The Portal

Bill Myers

A Division of Thomas Nelson Publishers
Since 1798

www.thomasnelson.com

Published in Nashville, Tennessee, by Tommy Nelson®, a Division of Thomas
Nelson, Inc. Visit us on the Web at www.tommynelson.com.

Scripture quotations are from the *International Children's Bible*®, *New Century
Version*®, copyright © 1986, 1988, 1999 by Tommy Nelson®, a Division of
Thomas Nelson, Inc.

Tommy Nelson® books may be purchased in bulk for educational, business,
fund-raising, or sales promotional use. For information, please e-mail us at
SpecialMarkets@ThomasNelson.com.

This is a work of fiction. Names, characters, places, and incidents either are the
product of the author's imagination or are used fictitiously.

Book design: Mark & Jennifer Ross / MJ Ross Design

ISBN 1-4003-0744-9

Printed in the United States of America
05 06 07 08 09 WRZ 9 8 7 6 5 4 3 2 1

For Brenda,
who believed in this series
more than any of us

Book 1
The Portal

CONTENTS

Book 1
The Portal

CHAPTER ONE

The Rock

It wasn't Denise's fault. It was just some weird rock she'd found in her uncle's attic. And what better gift to give a weird kid than a weird rock? How'd she know it would start to glow in her coat pocket? How'd she know by exposing it to the light of the full moon it would send out a distress call to some sort of "alternate dimension?" What'd she know about glowing rocks? Come to think of it, what did she know about alternate dimensions?

Now it's true, a rock for Nathan's birthday probably wasn't the best of gifts. Then again, Denise and Nathan weren't the best of friends. To say that she hated him might be an exaggeration. To say that at least once a week she had this deep desire to punch him in the gut, well, that at least would be the truth.

The problem was that Nathan was spoiled—big time. But it wasn't all his doing. Ever since the last operation—ever since the doctors said his hip would never be normal, that he'd always limp and have those sharp, jagged pains whenever he walked—Nathan was treated differently. And, being a fairly bright kid, Nathan did what any fairly bright kid would do. . . .

He milked it for all it was worth.

He milked it when he didn't want to go to school. He milked it when he didn't want to take out the trash. And he especially milked it to get whatever he wanted from his grandfather.

Yes, sir, Nathan knew all the tricks.

Denise rounded the corner and headed up the street toward Grandpa O'Brien's Secondhand Shop. That's where Nathan hung out when his folks were away on business. With any luck, his older brother, Joshua, might be there, too.

Good ol' Josh. A couple years older than Denise, he was always there for her. He was there to pull her off kids before she pulverized them in fist fights. He was there to help her with the math she could never quite master. He was even there when her father ran off. Denise was only four at the time and could barely remember what the man looked like. But she remembered Joshua. She remembered him playing with her and trying to make her laugh. And she'd never forget the time he held her when she couldn't stop crying. It made no difference how much the other kids teased him. He went right on holding her until she finally stopped.

Good ol' Joshua. Now if only his little brother could learn some of those traits.

As she moved up the sidewalk, Denise listened to the snow creaking and squeaking under her feet. She loved December nights—the way the stars were so close you could almost touch them, the way the store windows glowed with twinkling Christmas lights. She even loved the obnoxious ringing bell of the Salvation Army Santa Claus across the street.

Reaching the Secondhand Shop, she pushed open the door only to be knocked aside by two little kids racing out for all they were worth. Their reason was simple. Nathan and his grandfather were going at it again. . . .

"Grandpa, that's the third toy you've given away this week!"

"To be sure, lad, and don't you think I'd be knowing that?" The stout old man had come from Ireland almost forty years ago but still insisted on keeping his accent—and his temper.

Even at that, he was no match for Nathan's selfishness. The

The Rock

boy was a pro. Denise stood near the door watching the redheaded kid go after his grandfather with everything he had.

"Grandpa, how do you expect to make a profit?"

"Son, there's more to this life than making a—"

"You've seen the bank statements."

"Yes, lad, but—"

"You know what Mother's accountant said."

"Yes, but—"

"It's all there in black and white."

"I under—"

"If you don't start making a profit, you'll lose the store."

"Yes . . . but . . . I . . ." The old man was running out of steam. Denise could see him trying to change gears, searching for a new target. Unfortunately the one he chose happened to be Nathan's heart—an impossibly small mark for anyone to hit.

"It's the Johnson children," Grandpa sighed. "You know how they've always wanted a puppy. And since we got them little wooden pop-up ones last week, and since times have been so hard for . . ."

The old man slowed to a stop. The boy wasn't even listening.

Denise watched as Nathan hopped up on the stool behind the antique cash register. He spotted her and grinned, making it clear that this was all a game to him. A game she'd seen him play more times than she could count. And, if she guessed correctly, he was about to enter phase two of the game—the woe-is-me-self-pity phase.

"Times are hard for all of us, Grandpa." He glanced over at the stuffed toy on the counter beside him. It was an English bulldog complete with sagging wrinkles and floppy jowls. By the way it was left half unwrapped, it was obvious that it hadn't exactly met up to his high standards for birthday gifts.

Slowly he turned to his grandfather. One aspect of the self-pity phase was to make sure you either had a catch in your voice or a tear in your eye. Nathan had both. He was good. Very good.

"Oh, Grandpa, I don't mean to complain . . ." He threw in a couple sniffs for good measure. "But the Johnsons aren't the only ones who want a real dog."

"I know, son, but—"

"And if you're always giving stuff away so you don't have enough money . . . well . . ." He let his voice trail off into silent sorrow.

The old man bit his lip. It was obvious he loved the boy with all of his heart. "I'm sorry, lad. Maybe in a few months I'll be able to afford a nice puppy."

Nathan looked up and gave a brave nod.

Denise could see Grandpa's heart melting.

"But for now, this ol' bulldog here, he ain't a bad substitute, is he?"

Nathan managed to smile and get his bottom lip to tremble at the same time. Yes, sir, he knew all the moves.

Denise wasn't sure what was next, but she'd definitely seen enough. She stepped from the door and started toward the counter. "Hi, guys!"

"Oh, hi, Denny!" Grandpa exclaimed. "So how are you this fine winter evenin'?"

"Pretty good," she said. "So, where's Joshua? Still at basketball practice?"

"I believe so."

She turned to Nathan, who was giving her his famous death glare. She tried not to smile. Here he had gone to all this trouble getting Grandpa right where he wanted him and now she barged in completely ruining the mood. "Happy birthday, Nathan."

The Rock

"Thanks," he grumbled.

"I brought you a gift." She dug into her coat pocket.

"You did?" Suddenly he didn't sound quite so depressed.

"Yeah. It isn't much, but I think you'll like it." She pulled out the crimson-colored stone and plopped it down on the worn wooden counter.

Nathan stared at it blankly. "A rock?"

"Yeah, but not just any rock. I found it in my uncle's attic. Look at the cool red sparkles in it."

"Great," Nathan groaned as he picked it up. Obviously he didn't share her excitement. "A stupid stuffed dog . . . and now a rock. Some birthday." He tossed the stone back onto the counter where it rolled into a patch of moonlight that streamed in through the window.

"Nathan," Grandpa chided, "where are your manners?"

"Well, it's the truth, isn't it? Mom and Dad are off on some vacation—"

"Business," Grandpa corrected. "They're on a business trip."

"Whatever. And all you do is look out for everybody but me."

"Now, that's not true."

"Isn't it?" Nathan spun around and nailed Grandpa with another woe-is-me look. "What do you call it when you give away so much stuff that you can't afford to buy your own grandson the only present he's ever really wanted in his whole, entire life?"

Nathan scored a direct hit. Denise saw the guilt wash over Grandpa—guilt over giving the toy to the Johnson kids, guilt over not buying Nathan a real puppy, guilt over the boy's parents always being away. You name it, Grandpa was feeling guilty about it.

"All right, all right!" he exploded. He turned and headed for the cash register.

"What are you doing?" Nathan asked innocently.

Grandpa punched the buttons on the old machine and the money drawer rolled out. "You want a puppy? I'll be gettin' you a puppy!"

Nathan slipped Denise another smile as Grandpa grabbed the bills from the drawer, then turned to face him. "I'm takin' whatever money we got here and buyin' you your puppy!"

"But Grandpa," Nathan protested.

"No," the old man said as he stormed toward the coatrack and threw on his cap and scarf. "You've been whinin' and complainin' all week and I'll be havin' no more of it."

"But not all the money."

"I've made up my mind, lad." Grandpa slipped into his wool coat, hiked it up onto his shoulders, and headed for the door.

"Grandpa, please, not all your hard-earned—"

"No, sir," he said, yanking open the door and causing the little bell above it to jingle. "I'm goin' to Smalley's Pet Shop to buy you a puppy, and that's final!"

Just before Grandpa shut the door, Nathan was able to squeeze in one last protest. Well, it really wasn't much of a protest. "Make sure it's the black one with the white spots!"

The door slammed, once again jingling the bell, and the room fell silent.

Denise could only stare as Nathan broke into a grin. Finally, she was able to speak. "You—you had that all planned, didn't you?"

"Not the part about the rock," Nathan shrugged. "But that worked out pretty good, too, don't you think?"

Denise was stunned.

Nathan laughed. "Come on, lighten up. You'd do it too if you thought you could get away with it."

The Rock

"No way." Denise could feel the tops of her ears starting to burn like they always did when she got angry.

"Gimme a break," Nathan said. "Of course you would—we all would. That's the only way to get ahead in this ol' world—figure out what you want and go for it."

Sounding like some sort of professor with all the answers, he plopped his feet up on the counter and continued his lecture. Denise watched, both awed and repulsed.

"The way I see it, there are only two types of people . . ." He leaned back and clasped his hands behind his head. "The haves and the have-nots."

Once again she had this overwhelming urge to punch him in the gut. But this time something other than self-control stopped her. It was the rock. It had started to glow! It was filling with red, sparkling light. And the more Nathan talked, the brighter it grew—as if his words somehow gave it energy.

"You think billionaires get that way by looking out for the other guy?" he asked. "No sir. They get there by looking out for number one."

By now the glow was bright enough to light up the entire counter. Denise tried to shout, but she was too frightened to speak. She tried to back away, but she was too scared to move. So instead of shouting or backing away, she just stood there pointing.

But it didn't matter to Nathan. He wasn't looking. He was too busy giving his speech. Eyes closed and leaning back, he went on and on . . . and just when you thought he had finished, he went on some more.

All this as the red stone behind him continued to grow brighter and brighter, lighting up more and more of the room . . .

CHAPTER TWO

The Visitors

**Now hold it, partner,
that ain't how it's done.
If you're tryin' to be tops,
don't fight for number one.**

The voice sent Nathan and his stool crashing to the floor. One minute he was leaning back, lecturing Denise on the advantages of being selfish; the next minute he was on the ground shaking like a leaf.

"Who . . . who said that?" he stuttered.

Denise would have joined him in his demand but she was still trying to find her voice. Come to think of it, she was still trying to move. By now the entire room was filled with the rock's glaring red light. And that voice—that weird poetry—it seemed to come from everywhere. Every wall, every shelf, everything in the room vibrated with its sound.

"Where . . . where are you?" Nathan demanded with obviously false courage. (But right now, false courage was better than no courage.) He barely finished the words before the voice answered,

**Hold on to yer horses,
we'll be gettin' there soon.
Jes' need the right coordinates
to enter your room.**

The Visitors

Denise and Nathan exchanged looks of terror and astonishment.

The voice continued, this time talking to somebody else. "Got it this time, ol' buddy?"

An ultra-cool, gravelly voice answered, "Got it, do I."

"You sure?" the first voice asked. "Remember the last time when you—"

"Cool, is it," the second voice interrupted. "Got it, I do."

Next Denise heard four electronic sounds . . .

BEEP!........B^oP!........BLEEP!.......BURP!....

. . . followed by a "YEOOOWW!" as the door to the pot-bellied stove flew open and three very strange creatures leaped out. As they sailed through the air, they grew in size until they were nearly as tall as Denise and Nathan.

The first was a furry-faced bearlike fellow with a checkered vest and walking stick. But right now he wasn't doing much walking. With the seat of his pants on fire he was doing a lot more jumping and yelling. Most of that yelling was directed at the second creature, who was tall and purple with a foxlike face, long fluffy tail, and a large Mohawk. He was dressed in a tuxedo.

"Ow, ooo, ooch, ow, ow! Put me out! Quick, put me out!"

The purple creature did his best to slap out the flames. "Man, got it. It, I got." But he wasn't having the greatest success.

Nathan and Denise watched speechless as the strange dance continued—the furry creature running around with his pants on fire, the cool purple dude trying to put him out.

"Won't you, ooo, ooow, ever get them coordinates right?"

"Cool man, is it!"

After a few more attempts, the purple dude finally managed to smother the flames.

The furry creature sighed and gave a heartfelt, "Thanks."

"Cool," was all the cool dude said. Then suddenly remembering his own clothes, he began checking them urgently. "Coat my? Okay, is it?"

The furry creature looked over the cool dude's coat, brushed off a few ashes, then glanced at him with a grin. "Cool."

Relief swept over the purple creature's face.

With the preliminaries taken care of, they finally turned to face Denise and Nathan. For a moment all four stood in silence. There was no movement in the room—except, of course, for the slightest trace of smoke still rising from the furry creature's rear.

Nathan, who had managed to get back on his feet, was once again trying to sound brave (and might have succeeded if his voice wasn't shaking so much). "Who—who are you guys? Where'd you come from?"

The furry creature pulled himself together, straightened his tie, and answered,

> **So sorry about that.**
> **First, to answer your "who,"**
> **I'm Aristophenix T. Xanthrope,**
> **and this here is Listro Q.**

Denise glanced at Nathan. They may have got an answer, but it wasn't much help. She was about to step in and try a question of her own, when there was a sudden high-pitched squeal—like a tape recorder running at high speed.

They spun around and saw the third member of the party hovering behind them. At first glance, he looked like a dragonfly. On second glance, a ladybug. But neither dragonflies nor ladybugs have

The Visitors

glowing blue tails. This one did. He had a glowing blue tail that flickered and blinked for as long as he talked. He also wore glasses.

When he finally stopped talking, the cool dude nodded. "Taken, good point." Then turning back to Denise and Nathan, he introduced the third and final creature. "Here this is Samson."

Samson let out another long line of high-pitched chatter, which Denise naturally took as a greeting. Not wanting to appear frightened or impolite (like all those stupid earthlings in all those stupid sci-fi movies), she tried to smile graciously and answer the little fellow. "Well, thank you, and it's certainly a pleasure to meet you." In an effort to show universal friendship and politeness, she held out her hand to shake.

Samson immediately swooped down and bit it.

"Ow!" she yelled, pulling back her hand.

"Samson!" Listro Q scolded.

Aristophenix cleared his throat and tried to explain,

> **You'll have to excuse him,**
> **Sammy's not being rude.**
> **In Fayrah, opened hands**
> **mean you're offering food.**

"Fayrah?" Nathan asked. "What's that?"

"Home, for us," Listro Q answered.

"Yeah," Denise said, sucking her fingers, no longer quite so worried about universal friendship and politeness. "So why'd you come *here*?"

"Bloodstone threw you into moonlight." Listro Q motioned toward the rock Denise had given Nathan. It now sat on the counter just as plain and dull as any other rock.

"Bloodstone?" Nathan asked.

"Yes," Aristophenix said,

> A symbol to all,
> of Imager's great compassion,
> of the price that he paid,
> To bring you back into . . . uh . . . fashion!

Denise gave a little shudder. It had been a long time since she'd heard poetry quite so awful.

"A universal call for help made you," Listro Q said. "By putting it in moonlight."

"Help?" Nathan said. "We don't need any help."

"You don't?" Aristophenix asked, sounding a little disappointed.

"What do we need help for?" Nathan said.

"Selfishness, your speech?" Listro Q asked. "Number one looking out for, didn't just a minute ago hear we?"

"Huh?" Nathan asked.

Denise ventured a guess. "I think he's talking about your looking-out-for-number-one speech."

All three strangers nodded.

"Oh, you heard that?" Nathan asked, swelling with pride.

"Believe that, do you?" Listro Q asked.

"Well, yeah, sure."

"Then more help need you than know you."

Nathan frowned in confusion.

Aristophenix explained:

> In our world of Fayrah,
> the opposite is true.
> We care less for the me's,
> and far more for the you's.

The Visitors

Nathan broke out laughing. "Yeah, right." He looked back at the group.

Nobody was smiling.

"Come on." He gave a nervous chuckle. "Who are you fooling? No one could survive in a world where you care more for the other guy than for yourself. That's impossible."

Suddenly, all three creatures began to laugh.

"What?" Nathan demanded. "What's so funny?"

"Never wrong, more have been you."

Once again, Samson began to chatter.

Listro Q and Aristophenix listened carefully, throwing in a few "mm-hmm's" and "good's" until the little guy finally finished.

"What did he say?" Nathan asked.

Listro Q explained. "A child is still Samson. Graduate to adult-hood soon must he."

"Yeah?" Nathan said. "So what does that got to do with us?"

Aristophenix continued,

**To graduate in Fayrah,
good deeds Sammy must do.
So come over to our kingdom,
and let him show it to you.**

Nathan's face lit up. "You mean go with you? Like to another planet or something?"

Denise gave a little shiver and whispered, "Nathan."

"Actually," Aristophenix replied, "we call them *dimensions*."

"No kidding?"

"Nathan," Denise whispered louder.

He turned to her. "What?"

She wasn't sure how to say it without hurting anyone's feel-

13

ings, so she did what she did best. She just blurted it out. "We don't even know these . . . people."

"So?"

"So you just don't go along with a bunch of strangers . . . no matter what dimension they come from."

Nathan glared at her but Listro Q seemed to understand. "Correct, absolutely is she."

Aristophenix nodded, his furry face scrunched into a frown. "I understand what she's sayin', but—"

"Yes," Listro Q agreed, "however—"

"Exactly—," Aristophenix said.

"On the hand, other—"

"I see yer point, but—"

Samson joined in, long and loud.

Soon, Aristophenix was shouting to be heard.

So was Listro Q.

It had quickly turned into a free-for-all debate.

Denise and Nathan traded looks.

"Excuse me!" Nathan shouted.

No response, except for more arguing.

He tried again. "Excuse me! *Excuse me!*"

At last the three quieted down.

Somewhat embarrassed, Aristophenix pulled himself together, adjusted his tie, and answered,

> **We understand your fears.**
> **You are right, this we know.**
> **But to prove Nathan is wrong,**
> **our kingdom we really should show.**

"That's right," Nathan agreed.

The Visitors

Denise started to protest. "But—"

"Come on, Denny. Don't be such a chicken!"

Again she felt her ears starting to burn. "I am not a chicken!"

"Sure you are."

"No, I'm not, but—"

In a sudden burst of maturity, Nathan started clucking.

"Nathan," she warned.

He clucked louder.

"Knock it off!"

And louder still.

"Nathan!"

But he would not stop.

"Nathan, I'm warning you!"

Her warnings did no good. Finally, she'd had enough. You could call Denise a lot of things, but you couldn't call her a chicken. "All right, fine!" she shouted. "We'll go!"

Nathan grinned and the group nodded, pleased with her decision. Then she added, "But just for a few minutes."

Everyone agreed. But, even as they thanked her and promised her everything would be all right, Denise felt herself growing just a bit colder. She couldn't put her finger on it, but somehow she suspected this little trip of theirs would be anything but all right? . . .

◩

"Bobok, my precious and most trusted friend . . ." The Illusionist leaned forward on her throne, wrapping her leathery wings about her shimmering scales and war-scarred body. "Tell me on what occasion do you honor my humble kingdom with your wondrous presence?"

Bobok rolled back, just out of reach of her powerful hoofs. He knew she hated him almost as much as he hated her. In the past three thousand epochs, they had fought hundreds of battles over the disputed border between their two kingdoms. But now he had put all of that aside. Now he had come here, to Seerlo, the waterless kingdom of wind and sand, to speak with her personally.

"I sense a stirring in Imager's tapestry," he purred as he rolled from side to side in the fire-hot sand. He had lost all of his legs and arms in the Great Rebellion. And over the epochs of time, as he propelled himself by rolling, he had worn off all the other parts of his body as well. He had become a perfectly round orb—no nose, no ears, not even a head—just a perfectly round, ice-blue orb, with two tiny eyes set deep within their sockets. He continued. "Two threads are tugging at the Weave; two threads from the Upside-Down Kingdom are about to enter Fayrah."

"What?" the Illusionist asked in astonishment. "Don't they know it is still your season in Fayrah? Don't they know that you still have two hours in which to tempt anyone you can to cross through the Portal and enter your domain?"

"Perhaps they have forgotten," Bobok offered.

"And Imager, he would allow this?" she demanded. "After the awful price he has paid for their freedom? You _did_ say they were from the Upside-Down Kingdom."

Bobok smiled a sinister grin. "It is the supreme act of egotism, wouldn't you agree? Thinking his love would save them from our ways. But we must work together. If I succeed in wooing them through the Portal, I must cross your kingdom to reach mine."

"But of course, my kindest and dearest of friends. Whatever you wish. After all, it is your season. Of course there must be some minor charge—a tariff for such a crossing."

"Of course," Bobok softly agreed. "And what might that be?"

The Visitors

"Since we have been so close these many epochs, and since you are such a kind, handsome gentleman, the fee will be slight."

"I thought as much," Bobok cooed.

"Let me see," she thought aloud. "Your keen intellect perceived two threads, did it not?"

"Yes, male and female."

"And they've both been re-Breathed?"

"No, neither one has come to know Imager. Though the girl may be closer to re-Breath than the boy."

"Good . . . good—then you must let me try to lure the girl to stay with me."

"That is a hefty price, dear lady," Bobok protested, "to take half my catch."

In reply, the Illusionist gave the slightest wave of her hand. Instantly a thousand soldiers rose from underneath the sun-scorched sand. Part cockroach, part giant ant, they lay dormant to conserve their moisture until needed. Suddenly they scurried around Bobok, surrounding him on every side, buzzing their wings, clicking their pincer jaws, poised to attack.

But Bobok was not frightened. He had known this would be the Illusionist's response.

▣

She smiled sweetly—no easy task with a beak for a mouth—and spoke. "Surely a sensitive man of your great heart and giving nature would not deprive me of the girl."

"Of course not, gracious lady," Bobok purred. "The girl is as good as yours." With that he turned and started rolling through the hot sand, past the soldiers, and toward the distant Portal . . . toward the Kingdom of Fayrah.

He could practically hear the Illusionist grinning over her

17

powers of negotiation. But that was all right; he was grinning as well. It had gone exactly as he had planned. He had no interest in the girl—never had. All he wanted was the boy.

And he would do anything to get him.

CHAPTER THREE

The Journey Begins

"Denny, Bloodstone," Listro Q ordered. "Make sure, take it you."

Denise nodded and headed for the counter where the Bloodstone rested. Though she had carried it all the way to the Secondhand Shop, she was a little reluctant picking it back up. But when she finally took it into her hands, it felt as cool and normal as always.

She glanced at Listro Q, who was pulling a small electronic box from his pocket. It looked like a remote control to a TV, but somehow she suspected it did more than pick up local cable.

"Sure you got the coordinates right this time, ol' buddy?" Aristophenix asked.

"Cool, is it," came the reply.

Aristophenix nodded and turned to Nathan. "Will ya grab a couple of them canteens there on the back shelf for us?"

"Canteens?" Nathan asked skeptically.

"If ya don't mind."

Nathan shrugged and limped down the aisle to pick up a couple of old army surplus canteens.

Meanwhile, Aristophenix gave the final instructions,

> **To travel across dimensions,**
> **there's some things you must know,**
> **to help ease the trauma,**
> **and allow you to flow.**

"Most of the work, Cross-Dimensionalizer will do," Listro Q

said, referring to the little box in his hand. "But weight either have you of hate, anger, even unforgiveness, far too heavy to carry through the Center. Mind free of these burdens must be you."

"That's right," Aristophenix added.

**Think of things pleasant,
Imager has made,
the breadth of his passion,
which never will fade.**

Denise wasn't sure she completely understood, but she caught the general idea. Somehow the trip would be easier if she thought of happy things. No problem, she could handle that.

"Set everybody?" Listro Q asked.

Everyone nodded. Denise could feel her heart starting to pound in her chest. She took a deeper breath, forcing herself to relax. It didn't help.

Listro Q reached down to the control box, pressed four buttons . . .

BEEP!........BOP!........BLEEP!.......BURP!....

. . . and they were off.

Suddenly there was so much light that Denise couldn't see a thing. It was like looking into the sun. She closed her eyes, then squinted them open a crack until, slowly, gradually, she grew accustomed to the brightness. Only then did she notice that there were even brighter lights surrounding her. They were different shapes and every possible color imaginable, but they all had one thing in common. Like herself, they seemed to be traveling at incredible speed toward the middle of something.

The Journey Begins

We're falling, Denise thought. But there was no panic. Barely any fear. Instead, it was more of an observation. *We're all falling toward the center of something.*

Correct is that, Listro Q answered.

She turned and saw him directly beside her. Like the others he was also glowing. In fact, he was so bright that if it wasn't for his distinct shape, she might never have recognized him.

He continued to speak—but it really wasn't speaking because his mouth never moved. It was as if he was thinking the words and she somehow heard them. *All worlds and dimensions connected to the Center*, he explained. *Slow travel would it be around the outside from world to world. Faster travel is it through the Center.*

So we're going to the center of the universe? she asked.

Center of all universes. End and beginning of all things.

You mean like heaven or something?

Listro Q shrugged. *The Center—Imager's home is it. Imaged by him are all things—from him come all things.*

God? The Imager, is he like God?

Again Listro Q shrugged. *Intense pure—the Imager, is he. The Center, his home.*

Before Denise could ask any more questions, she spotted Aristophenix approaching. Like Listro Q, he glowed with brilliant light. Beside him little Samson also glowed. And beside him was what looked like the stuffed bulldog that had been sitting on the counter—the one that had been Nathan's birthday gift. Apparently the Cross-Dimensionalizer had sucked it up into their journey as well.

But what really startled Denise was Nathan—at least she thought it was Nathan. Yet this Nathan was full grown. Not only was he full grown, but he was incredibly handsome, and both of his legs were whole, his hip perfectly well. And his clothing? Instead of a sweater and jeans he now wore some sort of bright metal all over him, like a suit of armor.

In one hand, he held a shield. In the other, she noticed a couple canteens—the ones he'd picked up at the back of the store. But they were no longer canteens, not exactly. They'd changed their shape. Oh sure, they still had their black screw-on lids and the green camouflage cloth covers, but now they were shaped like . . . well, they almost looked like swords. And, on what would be the blades of those swords, there was the slightest spattering of . . . blood. But it wasn't human blood or even the blood of animals. Somehow Denise knew or felt that it was a different blood—like the blood of reptiles or maybe insects. *That's weird*, she thought, *insects don't have blood. Or do they?*

Aristophenix pointed toward the Center. They were approaching what looked like a thin layer of fog. And below that . . . below that was the outline of what could only be described as a city— but a city that glowed brilliantly!

Start thinking them good thoughts.
The Center we're nearer.
Keep thanking Imager,
so you'll pass freer and clearer.

Denise winced. The one thing that hadn't changed was Aristophenix's awful poetry. But she understood his warning and quickly searched her mind for something pleasant to be thankful for.

She had it. Toby, her cat. She thought of the first day her parents brought him home—an orange tabby kitten, all full of fluff and warmness. What wonderful feelings those were. She was only three or four at the time, but she recalled how both parents knelt

The Journey Begins

beside her, how they stroked Toby, how they smiled. Those were happy times—the best times.

The memory was so warm and tender that Denise barely noticed as they entered the Center—as the fog gently embraced and enfolded her. But, instead of cold and damp, this fog had the same warm, cuddly feelings as the kitten.

And then it happened. . . .

In her memory, she looked up to see her parents smiling. There was Mom, looking like she always did. And there was Dad. . . . But wait a minute. She couldn't see his face. There were his thick arms, his broad shoulders, even his wavy hair. But no face. Why couldn't she remember his face?

Then the anger started—a little at first, but it quickly grew. Anger over her parents' fights. Anger over his leaving. Anger over never seeing him again. Why? Why had he gone? What had she done? Why had he deserted her?

And, as the anger grew, the shaking began.

What's going on? she thought as she turned to her companions. But they were no longer beside her. They were several feet below, falling much faster and smoother.

For the first time since the journey began, Denise started to feel real fear. Cold, icy panic knotted her stomach. It quickly spread to the rest of her body. As it did, the shaking increased.

"*Listro Q!*" she shouted. "*Aristophenix?*"

But no one heard. No one noticed. Each was too immersed in his own thankfulness and joy.

Suddenly Denise felt alone. Alone and frightened. *Very* frightened.

As the fear grew, the shaking turned into violent lurchings and bouncings. She tried to scream but was thrown so savagely about that it was impossible to catch her breath. She clenched her teeth and closed her eyes—hoping through sheer concentration to ease the relentless shaking—to make whatever was happening stop. Again she tried to picture the kitten, but it did no good. There was too much fear now.

She noticed she was slowing. She was no longer falling as fast toward the Center. And the slower she fell, the less shaking she experienced, until both the shaking and her falling came to a stop.

But only for a moment.

Instantly, she was flung away—like a slingshot in the opposite direction, *away* from the Center. Faster and faster she flew. The lights and colors were a blur as she streaked past them. She looked down and spotted the Center. It quickly shrank to a little ball, then a little dot, then finally disappeared altogether. Now there was only the light. But even that was beginning to fade.

For the briefest moment, she was back in the Secondhand Shop—or thought she was. It came and went so quickly she wasn't sure. And then she entered a void—a hollow void that grew darker and darker.

Help me! she tried to scream. But she was going so fast the words were sucked from her mouth before she could shout them. The darkness increased, growing blacker and blacker, until there was no light at all. Nothing. Total darkness. There was no up, no down, only speed, terrifying, horrifying speed, hurtling her deeper and deeper into the blackness.

Then she saw them. She gasped. How could it be? How, in this total darkness, was there a blacker darkness? But not just one. Hundreds of them. Hundreds of black shadows racing through the darkness. Shadows feeding upon the darkness, devouring the existing darkness, sucking it into themselves and creating an oblivion so deep, so intense, that reality itself seemed to disappear.

The Journey Begins

Sensing her presence, they began turning in her direction. Then, to her horror, they started racing directly at her!

Denise threw out her hands to protect herself, though she couldn't even see those hands. She couldn't see anything. To be honest, she wasn't even sure if she was still alive. Of course she was alive. Why else would she feel so dizzy? Why else would she hear the pounding of her heart in her ears?

The shadows continued their approach from all sides. But that wasn't true, there were no sides. There was nothing.

The pounding in her ears grew deafening. Her head spun so fast that she could no longer think. *So this is what dying feels like,* was her last thought as she began losing consciousness. That and, *Are those Daddy's eyes?* For, suddenly, she was staring directly into her father's dark eyes. Well, they were his eyes, yet somehow they weren't. For these eyes looked like they understood every hurt, every sorrow, and every heartbreak she had ever had.

And then there was nothing

CHAPTER FOUR

Arrival

At first the voices were a blur. Soft, velvet murmurings that floated above what sounded like a distant bubbling brook.

"Hold it, partner. It looks like she's comin' around."
"How tell, can you?"

Her eyes are a twitchin',
they're startin' to move.
It looks like her condition,
is 'bout to improve.

Denise struggled to open her eyes, but they were just too heavy.

"Come on, darlin', you can do it—jes' concentrate."
"Minute now, any . . ."

The voices were much clearer, but she still couldn't understand the words. It sounded like they were talking a foreign language. But it was more than that. She wasn't certain, but they were definitely talking strange—very strange.

So take that there water skin,
and put it to her lips.
She won't understand,
till you give her some sips.

Arrival

Denise felt her head being lifted and the cool rim of a container placed against her mouth. Instinctively, she opened up and took a swallow. It was wet and cool and perfect. Just what she needed.

"Careful, my good man. Not too much at first."

"And don't be forgettin' her ears."

Denise felt her head tilted to one side. She was more than a little startled as several drops of the cold liquid splashed into her ear. Then her head was tilted to the other side as more was splashed into the other ear.

"It's no fair making the rest of us wait till she gets better. Can't somebody just stay with her while we go check out the place?"

Suddenly Denise understood everything. Every word, every sentence—she even recognized that last voice. It belonged to the one and only Nathan More-Spoiled-Than-Any-Brat-She-Knew O'Brien.

"Patience, partner, patience," Aristophenix's voice said.

"Actually, Master Nathan, the greater number of amiable faces surrounding her at the time of consciousness will facilitate a swifter recovery, thereby allowing you to see the kingdom as quickly and as unimpaired as possible."

But whose voice was that? Denise had no idea. And since lying around and listening to voices was not exactly how she wanted to spend her time, she mustered up more strength. Focusing all of her concentration upon her eyelids, she was finally able to pry them open.

"Ah, there go we," Listro Q said, looking down at her. He was at her left with Samson hovering just over his shoulder. On the other side she saw Aristophenix kneeling and looking just as chubby and dapper as ever. And beside him, with his head kind of upside down, was Nathan. Much to her disappointment, it was the old Nathan—the spoiled, whining Nathan. What happened to the other one—with the shining armor and mighty swords? Had it been a dream?

"I do believe, Master Nathan, that the female will soon be as spry as ever."

It was the new voice again. Denise looked above her head and was astonished to see the stuffed bulldog peering down at her. She was even more amazed when he gave a stiff, stodgy cough and continued speaking!

"Note the color already returning to the cheeks, as well as—"

A stuffed animal speaking! What's going on? she thought.

"So is she going to be okay or what?" Nathan demanded. "I got things I want to see here."

Good old Nathan. Some things never change. With that strange and somewhat comforting thought, Denise struggled to sit up.

"Girl now, cool be," Listro Q cautioned.

By now everything had cleared and focused for her. Everything except Nathan. For some reason his face still remained upside down.

She tried to speak, but the words came out dry and choking.

"Water, more have some," Listro Q encouraged as he lifted the water skin to her mouth. She took a small sip, but soon found herself gulping in as much as she could. She had never tasted anything quite so good or satisfying.

"Now, easy, easy," Listro Q warned as he gently pulled the water skin away.

After taking a moment to catch her breath, Denise finally spoke. "What . . . what happened?"

"Enter you could not the Center," Listro Q answered. "Vibrate with thanks, all created things. Not, did you."

Arrival

Confused, she turned to Aristophenix who explained,

> From rocks to trees,
> to stars to man,
> to vibrate thanks
> is our purpose and plan.
> By refusing to join
> or not knowing how,
> nowhere in his presence
> did Imager allow.

"Oh, so this was all his fault—that Imager guy."

"For your own protection was it," Listro Q explained.

"Yeah, sure," she scorned. "Some protection."

"Your vibration, your frequency out of phase. Kill you would it. By forbidding entrance, save you, did he."

"Right," she scoffed. Already memories flooded in faster than she cared to remember. Memories of the Center and the awful shaking, memories of the terrifying darkness . . . and memories of those eyes . . . those sensitive, pain-filled eyes. Eyes that seemed to be her father's but were somehow deeper.

"Who caught me, then?" she demanded. "Who saved me?"

"Saved you?" Listro Q asked.

"Well, yeah, how did I get here?"

Aristophenix glanced at the others. He nervously cleared his throat and tried to explain.

> As best we can figure,
> you went the long way 'round.
> And doing it by yourself
> makes it more than profound.

"But my dad, didn't you see him?" Denise asked. "He's the one who caught me. Didn't you see him?"

"Denny," Nathan sighed impatiently, "your dad hasn't been around for years. You know that."

"Well, yeah," she faltered, "but it looked like him . . . except for the eyes. And what about you?" She turned to Nathan. "You just made it through there without any sweat?"

"Not at first."

Denise looked at him, waiting for more.

"I tried singing a bunch of songs—you know, happy stuff— but nothing seemed to work. I just kept getting knocked around harder and harder."

"Tell me about it," Denise said.

"Then I remembered one of Grandpa's hymns from Ireland— one he always sang to me at bedtime . . ." His voice trailed off as if he were lost in thought, as if he'd experienced something he could not quite explain.

"And?" Denise persisted.

He came to. Then he simply shrugged. "And here I am."

Denise's frustration grew. "What about all that armor you were wearing?"

He looked puzzled. "Armor?"

"Yeah, you were dressed in some sort of weird getup with swords and—"

"I was dressed weird?" Nathan said defensively.

"Well, not weird. Actually you looked kinda—"

"What about you in that wedding dress?"

"Wedding dress?" It was Denise's turn for surprise.

"And how did you get it to glow like that?" he asked. "You looked pretty cool." Then, catching himself, he added, "I mean,

Arrival

considering how stupid you normally look."

Denise was so puzzled she barely noticed the put-down. What wedding dress was he talking about? And why hadn't he noticed the armor he was wearing? Things were definitely strange. On the bizarre scale of one to ten, this was definitely pushing an eleven.

Suddenly Samson began to chatter.

"Right are you," Listro Q agreed. "To see much have we." Turning to Denise he asked, "Walk, you think can you?"

"Of course I can," she said.

With the help of the others, Denise started to rise to her feet. She wished she hadn't.

There was a loud *whooshing* sound and immediately she found herself standing upside down. Well, it really wasn't standing . . . her feet shot straight up toward the sky and her head rested firmly on the ground.

"What's going on?" she screamed.

"Don't panic," Nathan said.

"Yeah, right, like this happens all the time!" She threw a look at Nathan and was surprised to see that he was also upside-down. But they were the only ones. Everybody else seemed to be standing perfectly normal.

"This is crazy!" she yelled.

Nathan answered, "They say it's because we're from the Upside-Down Kingdom."

"Upside-Down what?"

"Kingdom. They say our world is the only world in the universe that does things upside down."

"Upside down?" she repeated. Not only was she angry, but she was doubly upset that Nathan seemed to be taking it so calmly. "What do they mean, upside down?"

"In our world if you want stuff you take it," Nathan said. "Or if you want to be like the boss or leader, you make sure everyone else obeys you."

"So?"

"So here," he continued, "if you want something you give it away, or if you're trying to be the leader, then you help others."

"That's crazy!"

"No . . . just upside-down."

"For them!" Denise sputtered. "They're the ones that are upside-down—not us!"

"I guess," he shrugged. "Except for one little thing."

"What's that?"

"We're the ones standing on our heads."

Denise looked back at the group. "Great," she groaned, "so we spend the rest of our time here just standing on our heads."

"I say there . . . I do believe there is an expedient solution available." It was the bulldog again.

"And why aren't you upside-down?" Denise demanded. She didn't mean to be so cranky, but all in all it hadn't been one of her better days. And at the moment, it didn't seem to be getting any better. "If you're from our world, why aren't you flipped around like us?"

"Obviously, my dear human, because I don't have the potential of being Imager-Breathed."

"Oh great, more of this Imager stuff. He really knows how to show his guests a good time, doesn't he?"

"Get real," Nathan sighed. "We're not in the Center anymore. We passed through it to get to Fayrah."

"My dear Master Nathan . . ." The dog cleared his throat. "If you would be so kind as to allow me to continue?"

Arrival

"Certainly, Mr. Hornsberry," Nathan said.

"Mr. Hornsberry? What a name." Denise muttered. "Doesn't that just figure."

Ignoring her, the dog continued. "In my humble estimation, I believe your dilemma is an optical phenomenon." He turned to Listro Q and Aristophenix. "Am I correct, gentlemen?"

They both nodded.

"Then, by simply placing a few drops of your special water into their eyes—as you have already done with their ears, allowing them to hear right side up—will they not also be able to see right side up?"

"Mr. Hornsberry, you're a genius!" Nathan shouted.

The dog coughed slightly. "Yes, well, that goes without saying, doesn't it?"

"If that's all it takes, let's get on with it!" Denise demanded.

"Patience, female, patience," Mr. Hornsberry scolded. "Why you humans were ever given control is beyond me." He turned to Listro Q and asked, "My good man, would you be so kind as to do us the honors?"

"Cool," Listro Q said as he opened his water skin and knelt down to the faces of Nathan and Denise. "Your eyes, open keep you. Lots of water into them let you."

They nodded.

Listro Q poured the water into his hands. It was the first time Denise had seen it. Oh, she had tasted it, all right, with all its cool goodness. She'd even felt it as they poured it into her ears. But seeing it for the first time was quite a shock. Because it wasn't water at all! Well, maybe it was. Who could tell in this place? But what it looked like was . . . letters and words. That's right, liquid letters and words. It was as if someone had taken the alphabet and somehow managed to turn it into liquid. There was an **S** pouring out, followed by a **W**, then an **L**. Next came an entire word, ***THE***, followed by ***BEHOLD***, and ***in***, and a half dozen more. Though they were all shapes and sizes, there was no missing the fact that they were actual letters and words pouring into Listro Q's hand.

All Denise could do was stare.

With his hand cupped full of the liquid, Listro Q said, "Go, here we!" and quickly splashed it into Nathan's face.

For a moment, nothing happened. But as soon as he opened his eyes, as soon as some of the liquid fell into them, Nathan was standing right side up with the rest of them.

"All right, way to go!" the group cheered as they slapped Mr. Hornsberry on the back and congratulated Nathan.

"Excuse me . . . ," Denise called. "*Excuse me?*" Finally she managed to get their attention. "I don't mean to be rude or anything, but do you think maybe you could get around to doing me?"

"Certainly," Listro Q said as he kneeled back down to join her. He poured out another handful of the liquid letters and, without warning, quickly splashed them into her face. There was the loud *whooshing* sound again, and when she opened her eyes, she was also standing right side up.

There was more congratulating and backslapping, but Denise barely heard. She was too taken by the beauty. . . .

Aristophenix saw her expression and softly spoke,

> **Welcome to Fayrah,**
> **the kingdom of love,**
> **where the harshest assault**
> **is the cooing of doves.**

Arrival

Denise didn't know about that, but she did know it was the most beautiful place she had ever seen. . . .

First there were the colors. They were the same as back home, but somehow richer, more vivid. Yet none of them were too bright or glaring. Instead, each color gently blended into the next. Everything had its own distinct color and outline, yet each of those colors and outlines blended gently and naturally into its neighbor. It reminded her of a soft watercolor painting.

Then there were the trees. They were everywhere, each having their own shade of glimmering green leaves—leaves that she suspected would never fall, and if they did, somehow they would never need to be raked—at least not by girls who had better things to do on Saturday afternoons.

Past the trees were rolling hills—jade green and as soft as velvet. And past the hills, well past the hills, was something Denise had never seen before—mountains. But instead of the usual purple or violet hues, these mountains were a faint and very pleasant shade of . . . red. Not only that, but they seemed to be softly glowing and pulsating.

"Look!" She pointed.

"Ah, the Blood Mountains." Aristophenix nodded.

"Bloodstone from these mountains came yours," Listro Q said.

Remembering she still had the stone in her pocket, Denise pulled it out to take a look. Much to her surprise, it was glowing again. Glowing and pulsating in exact rhythm to the mountains!

"Neat," Nathan said as he tried to reach for it—until Denise blocked him. It may have been *his* gift, but right now *she* was holding it.

"Celebration signal to all," Listro Q explained as he motioned to the mountains, "that arrived here have Upside Downers."

"What?" Denise asked.

"Because here visiting are you, glow in celebration do the mountains."

"You mean those mountains are glowing like that just 'cause we're here, visiting?"

Listro Q nodded silently.

"Why?"

Listro Q smiled. "Upside Downers very precious are to Imager." Then turning back to the mountains, he continued, his voice lowering in reverence. "The Great Purchase . . . mountains these, reminder are they."

"Great Purchase?" Denise asked.

"Yes. Of Upside Downers."

A stillness crept over the group as everyone looked on in a gentle sense of awe. Well, almost everyone . . .

"Hey, everybody, take a look!"

Since Nathan couldn't hold the Bloodstone or be the center of attention, he had focused on something else. Denise turned to see him pointing at a stream a dozen yards behind them. But it wasn't a stream of water, it was a stream of those letters and words.

Aristophenix turned to him.

> **Thank you, dear Nathan,**
> **I'd almost forgot,**
> **you must fill your canteens,**
> **so truth can be sought.**

"Alright!" Nathan cried as he grabbed the canteens and quickly limped toward the stream.

Of course, Denise wanted to talk more about the Blood Mountains and the Bloodstone. But since Nathan had found another topic, and since Nathan loved to control the conversa-

Arrival

tions, it was clear that she'd have to wait. She shook her head in mild frustration. Good ol' Nathan.

"Check it out!" he called.

The others had turned to join him. Denise started to follow, then felt a strange sensation. She slowed to a stop. Was somebody watching them? She turned and looked. Nobody was there. Just the shimmering grass, the jade green trees, and the—wait a minute, what was that? Behind those bushes? Something blue.

Denise shaded her eyes from the sun for a better look. It was about the size of a soccer ball and it glistened in the light like glass or—could it be . . . *ice*?

Yes, *blue ice*.

She lowered her hand and was about to investigate when Nathan shouted, "Denny!"

She turned to see him standing at the bank of the stream. "Come on!" he yelled. "You gotta see this!"

She hesitated, then turned back to the bushes. But it was gone. The little blue ball had disappeared.

"Come on!" Nathan shouted.

She looked in every direction, but it was nowhere to be seen. How strange. How very strange.

"Denny!"

She turned back to him.

"Will you come on!"

Finally, with a heavy sigh, Denise turned and headed off to join him.

CHAPTER FIVE

The Stream

"Is this cool or what?!" Nathan shouted as he dropped to the grassy bank and began untying his shoes.

"You're not going in there!" Denise cried in alarm.

"Sure, why not?" He'd already kicked off his shoes and was working on his socks. "We drank the stuff and it didn't kill us. And Listro Q splashed it all over our faces."

Denise turned back to Listro Q and Aristophenix. "Is it really safe?" she asked.

"Perfectly." Aristophenix smiled as he waddled closer to the stream.

"'Sides," Nathan called, peeling off his shirt, "I can't wait to tell Mrs. Barnick, my English teacher, that I took a dip in her precious alphabet. Maybe she'll finally give me an *A* this time."

Listro Q turned to Denise. "Welcome are you, to join him."

"I don't think so," she said, giving a dubious look at the stream. Call her old-fashioned, but somehow she felt words and letters were better suited for reading than for jumping in and swimming with.

But not Nathan. With a slapping splash, he dove headfirst into the words and disappeared.

Denise watched and waited, but he didn't resurface. She glanced at the others. No one seemed concerned. She tried to relax. *He'll be up any minute*, she assured herself. *After all, didn't Aristophenix just say it was safe? And if Aristophenix said it was safe, it was safe.*

Or was it? Seems her little cross-dimensional trip hadn't been so safe. Come to think of it, it had been downright dangerous.

The Stream

Let's go, Nathan, she thought. *Don't be a jerk. Come back up.*

But Nathan didn't come back up.

The inside of Denise's palms grew damp. It's true, the two of them weren't exactly the best of friends, but Nathan was a human being (though there were times she had her doubts). Besides, what would she tell Joshua, his older brother, if something happened? "Hey, sorry 'bout losing your brother back in that other dimension, but, like, can we still be friends?"

Come on, Nathan, come back up!

She looked to the group. Maybe these creatures weren't so interested in their safety after all. Maybe this was all an elaborate trap, some way to lure poor unsuspecting earth kids into another world so they could be kidnapped and drowned. When you got right down to it, how long had she known them? Basically, weren't they just your common, average, run-of-the-mill strangers? Well, all right, maybe furry faces, purple skin, and glowing tails weren't exactly run-of-the-mill, but they were still strangers. And what did every kid know about taking rides with strangers?

What have we done?!

Her mind raced for a solution. *I could jump in there and save him. Yeah! Before they stopped me, I could kick off my shoes and leap in there to save his life! 'Course I can't swim, but—*

Suddenly, there was a stirring on the surface of the words.

Finally—he's coming up!

Wrong again. It was just a breeze rippling across the water's surface. Denise was definitely in a panic. And for good reason.

Then, just when she was about to jump back, point her finger, and blow the whistle on them—just when she was ready to challenge them to one of her world-famous fistfights, Nathan exploded from the surface laughing and gulping for air.

Denise was furious . . . and relieved.

"This is incredible!" he shouted. "Denny, there's no bottom to this thing!"

At first she was going to give him a good lecture. But what good would a lecture do? He'd just laugh and make her feel foolish—something she was becoming an expert at. By now she was sure everyone considered her the group idiot—first with her cross-dimensional detour, then her little stand-on-the-head routine. No, she'd been enough of a fool for one day, thank you very much.

So instead of giving Nathan the lecture he deserved, she tried to smile. She pretended to be Denise I'm-Having-a-Good-Time kid, instead of the Denise I-Know-We're-All-Going-to-Die fool.

She watched as the words **THEREFORE**, *surely*, and **BEGAT** dripped from Nathan's hair. They fell to his shoulders and slid down his back before splashing into the stream where they swirled around his waist and disappeared.

Trying her best to sound calm and matter-of-fact, she turned to Aristophenix and asked, "So where does the stream come from?"

"The Center," Aristophenix answered.

> **It comes to Fayrah**
> **and wanders around,**
> **for us to employ**
> **when truth must be found.**

"But the words, the letters?" she asked.

"Imager's mouth, come from they," Listro Q answered. "Every word, every sentence, spoken by him."

"Hey, Denny, check it out!" Nathan squirted a handful of water at her. The word **PEACE** shot from his closed palms and landed

The Stream

on the bank just a few feet from her. She watched as it slowly seeped into the ground and disappeared.

Samson briefly chattered.

"Right," Listro Q agreed. "More to see much. Nathan! Come must you!"

"Ah, do we have to?"

"Come," he repeated. Then, stooping down, Listro Q grabbed the two canteens Nathan had left on the bank and handed them to Denise. "Filled must be these."

She took them and moved to the edge of the bank. *Typical*, she thought. *Nathan gets to play while I do all the work.* But the thought didn't last long. For when she knelt down and looked into the stream, she was in for another surprise. It wasn't the letters and words that startled her; it was her reflection. A reflection that wasn't her. Well, it was her and it wasn't. It did everything she did. It gasped when she gasped. It moved when she moved. But the reflection was of a much older Denise. And, she had to admit, a much more beautiful one.

There was something else above the reflection. It wore a breathtakingly gorgeous wedding gown. Intricately embroidered, it had long lacy sleeves and a sparkling veil made of tiny pearls—pearls so fine and shimmering that they could have been morning dew on a spider's web. Slowly, she raised her hand toward her face, to touch the veil. But of course there was no veil there. It existed only in the reflection.

Then she saw Listro Q's reflection over her shoulder, smiling. Unlike her, he looked exactly the same as in real life.

"I don't—I don't understand," she said, unable to take her eyes from the stream.

"Imager's words, show reality—things as they are, not as they appear."

"But . . . that's not me, that's not what I look like."

"You how Imager sees."

"But that . . ." She motioned to the reflection. "That's not real."

Listro Q chuckled softly and pointed at her reflection. "More real that . . ." He pointed to her. "Than ever will be this."

"Come on, Denny, are you going to fill those canteens or what?" Suddenly her reflection shattered into a million pieces as Nathan splashed through it to reach the shore. "Here, gimme one of those." He grabbed a canteen from her hand and quickly dipped it into the water.

"Quite so, Master Nathan," Mr. Hornsberry said in his typical snooty manner. "If one doesn't take charge, one may never accomplish anything."

"You got that right, Hornsey," Nathan said, pulling the filled canteen from the stream and grabbing the next one from Denise. "Especially when all some people want to do is sit around and gawk at themselves."

Denise would have fired off a stinging comeback, especially after the fright he'd given her with his little drowning imitation. But she didn't say a word. All she could do was stare at the reflection as it reformed.

Only now it wasn't just her reflection, it was also Nathan's—the older Nathan—the one wearing the glowing suit of armor and carrying the shield and bloodstained swords. But it was more than just the armor that surprised her. It was those eyes. His eyes. Sure, his mouth was busy spouting the usual sarcasm and put-downs, but the eyes, they were different. In the reflection they appeared kind . . . even sensitive.

In his haste Nathan never saw the reflections. "Come on, let's get out of here," he said as he rose to his feet with the second canteen. "We've got lots to see."

The Stream

Denise continued to stare.

"Denny, are you coming? Denny?"

Slowly she rose to her feet. She hesitated a moment and looked back at the stream a final time. Her reflection remained, as if waiting. But waiting for what?

"Heads up!"

She turned just in time to catch one of the canteens Nathan had thrown at her.

"Carry your own water," he scorned. "I'm not your slave." With that he turned and started limping up the path. The rest of the group joined him. Reluctantly, Denise followed.

Then, as if to remind everyone of their mission (and that he was in charge of it), Aristophenix raised his walking stick and cheerfully spoke.

> **To show you Fayrah**
> **is our purpose and plan,**
> **how different we live**
> **from the species of Man.**

They'd only traveled for a few moments before Samson hovered over Nathan's head and chattered something.

"What's that?" Nathan asked.

It was Mr. Hornsberry's time to translate. "Master Nathan, I do believe he is referring to your shoes. In your admirable effort to hurry the female, you have forgotten your shoes."

Nathan looked down. "Oh, man," he complained. "It's this stupid path. The grass is so soft I forgot I wasn't wearing them. I gotta go back. You guys keep going, I'll catch up in a second."

"Back, go can we all," Listro Q offered.

"No way," Nathan said. "If Denny gets to looking at herself in the water again, there's no telling when we'll be able to leave."

The group chuckled.

Denise bit her lip.

"Over this knoll just, is the Capital," Listro Q said, pointing to the grassy hill in front of them. "Wait, can we."

"Go ahead," Nathan said as he started back. "I'll meet you there."

"Wait for me, Master Nathan," Mr. Hornsberry called as he scampered after the boy. "I shall accompany you!"

"Are you sure, ol' buddy?" Aristophenix called one final time.

"You go ahead," Nathan insisted. "We'll catch up."

▣

Eventually, Nathan found his shoes, slipped them on, and plopped down on the side of the stream to tie them. And it was there, for the first time since he'd entered Fayrah, that he felt a chill. Strange, he'd never paid attention to the temperature before, probably because the climate was so perfect—not too hot, not too cold. But now he felt a definite shiver creeping across his shoulder blades. He threw a glance at Mr. Hornsberry, who sat beside him. By the way the dog flared his nostrils, he'd also sensed something in the air. Then, suddenly, there was a voice. . . .

"Greetings, most favored."

Nathan gave a start. But he wasn't frightened. Maybe because the voice was so smooth and gentle that it almost sounded like his own thoughts. He turned and saw a little blue sphere near him. It was about the size of a soccer ball and was gently rolling back and forth. It had no arms, no legs, not even a nose or ears—just two deeply recessed eyes, and a mouth.

"Who—who are you?" Nathan asked.

"My name is not important. You are the only one of importance."

44

The Stream

Mr. Hornsberry rose from his haunches and gave a low growl.

"Easy, Hornsey, it's okay," Nathan said. He reached out to pat him on the head and Mr. Hornsberry relaxed slightly. Pats on the head are good for a dog's relaxation—even haughty, intellectual ones. Turning back to the orb, Nathan asked warily, "Why am I so important? What did I do?"

"It's not what you did," the blue sphere purred, "it's who you are. You are one of Imager's chosen. A brilliant thread in his nearly perfect tapestry."

Nathan eyed the sphere carefully as it rolled closer. The chill grew deeper.

"But a thread not allowed to rise to its fullest potential . . ."

"What—what do you mean?" Despite the chill, Nathan found himself strangely attracted to the creature.

"Have you never felt you were different—that somehow you were better than others?" The attraction increased with every word. "That you were somehow . . . *special*?"

"Well—well, yes," Nathan stuttered, "how did you know?"

"Because it is truth and I know truth." The creature turned to Mr. Hornsberry. "And you, my little friend—how clever you are to see your master's greatness."

Whatever concerns Mr. Hornsberry had, seemed to disappear. The stranger's words were as comforting as any pat on the head. "Well, yes." The dog nervously cleared his throat. "I am rather, as you say, *clever*, aren't I?" He gave his stubby tail a wag.

The creature grinned. He rolled closer to Nathan but kept a wary eye on the stream. Something about the water seemed to make him nervous. "When I speak of your greatness, oh, Chosen Thread, don't you feel a stir of excitement? Does not your heart beat a little faster at the hearing of this truth?"

It was true. All of his life Nathan had felt that he was somehow different—special. He thought it when he saw the rock stars onstage or the movie stars on the screen. That should be him up there. He could do that. If he only had the right breaks, he could be as great as any of them. Even better. He was sure of it. And now . . . could it be? Could all of those thoughts, those feelings, could they really be true?

"Listen to your instincts," the sphere cooed as it rolled even closer. "Trust them, trust what your heart whispers as truth."

"But . . . ," Nathan asked hoarsely, "I don't understand. How—how do I, you know, become . . . great?"

The creature chuckled. "You already are great—you simply have not experienced it."

"But . . ."

"Come, follow your humble servant to his kingdom."

"You mean a different kingdom than this one?"

The creature rolled back and forth in a gentle nod.

"Why?"

"To rule."

"What?"

"We have been waiting many epochs for your arrival. You are one of the great, a chosen thread."

Nathan's thoughts swam. Was such a thing possible?

"Surely this call to greatness does not surprise you. Listen to your heart, listen to its stirrings. Inside, you know you have been called to it."

"But—but what about Listro Q and Aristophenix . . . and Samson. They invited me to see *their* kingdom."

The sphere rolled so close that Nathan could now feel the coldness of its breath. It said only one word. "Why?"

The Stream

Nathan was having a harder time concentrating. The stranger had filled his head with so many thoughts that he was thinking of everything and nothing all at the same time. "I don't . . . know . . . ," he stuttered. "Something about giving, about serving."

The blue sphere broke into laughter. "Don't you see, that is simply another trick to deprive you."

"Deprive me?"

"Yes, just as your hip has deprived you for so many years."

Instinctively Nathan reached down to touch his leg. The stranger had spoken another truth. He could do so much. He could be so great. If it just wasn't for his stupid hip.

"Do you think Imager wanted you to have that deformity?" The orb pressed in. "Not at all. It was thrust upon you to deprive you, to prevent you from finding your true self, from becoming all you were meant to be."

Nathan's heart pounded harder and faster.

The orb continued, "If you visit Fayrah and learn only to give and serve, you will never rise to your true stature of greatness. It is another merciless trick to deprive you of your destiny."

"My destiny?"

"Come with me, Chosen Thread. Mine is a different kingdom—a kingdom of owners. Only the weak are destined to give. You are destined to take. You are destined to possess. In my kingdom, everything your eyes behold can become yours. No longer will you be deprived. No longer will your destiny be hindered. You will become exactly what you have been chosen to be since the beginning of time."

With that the orb turned and started rolling away from the stream. "Come . . . follow your trusted servant. Follow him. Your kingdom awaits."

"But where is it?" Nathan asked as he jumped up and limped to join him. Mr. Hornsberry trotted excitedly at his side. "What is the name of this special kingdom?"

"Keygarp," the sphere said as he continued forward.

"And your name, you never told me your name."

The sphere turned toward him and purred ever so gently. "My name . . . Bobok."

CHAPTER SIX

The Capital

Denise wasn't sure what to expect as they neared the top of the knoll. Except for Listro Q, Aristophenix, and Samson, she hadn't seen one other person from Fayrah. Granted, everything else in this world was beautiful—the trees, the hills, the glowing mountains, even that peculiar stream. But what about the people?

The question was short-lived. For as they reached the top of the hill, the valley came into view. And nestled in that valley was the Capital of Fayrah.

It was breathtaking. Magnificent. And even more surprising was the fact that it wasn't surprising. Not to Denise. Not anymore. Somehow she'd expected breathtaking magnificence. And she was not disappointed. She saw it in the quaint cottages, the emerald green lawns, the perfectly manicured trees and shrubs . . . and most importantly, she saw it in the people—lots of happy, laughing, slap-you-on-the-back kind of people.

Well, maybe *people* wasn't exactly the right word. . . .

Not only were there several of the Aristophenix and Listro Q varieties, but there were also dozens of even stranger and weirder types. Yet, even though the shapes and sizes were strange and weird, they weren't frightening. Like everything else in Fayrah, they were incredibly unique and yet perfectly blended.

Then there were the buzzing dragonflies or ladybugs or whatever they were—the ones that looked like Samson. Hundreds of these little critters zipped about chattering a mile a second. More than a few buzzed around the group to check them out. It was then that Denise realized they weren't exactly like Samson. All the others had beautiful sparkling tails that glowed a pleasant red, like the Blood Mountains. But, for some reason, Samson's tail was the only one that glowed blue. Although it wasn't an ugly blue, it certainly wasn't red like all the others.

Poor thing, she thought. *Even in a place like this I bet it's no fun being the oddball.* And Denise knew exactly what that felt like— being the oddball. . . .

—If she's so smart on those I.Q. tests, how come she's so dumb in school?

—What's a pretty girl like that trying to prove by beating up all those boys?

—Lots of kids don't have fathers. Why does she make such a big deal about it?

Denise had heard the questions whispered behind her back for years. And since no one ever had the answers, that made her, what else, but the *oddball.*

"Well, bless my soul, is this the Upside Downer?"

Denise turned to see a camel-type creature. It wore a large hoopskirt and had two furry arms extending from its chest. At the moment it was reaching out those arms for a hug. Unsure what to do, Denise looked at Listro Q, who gave a nod. With more than a little hesitancy, she moved over to hug the creature.

"It's certainly a privilege to be makin' your acquaintance." The camel spoke in a charming Southern drawl while hugging Denise so enthusiastically that Denise could hardly breathe. "My name is Sally."

"How do you do . . . Sally? I'm Denise."

"What a charming name," the camel creature said, pulling back. "Will you all be staying long?"

"Not long," Aristophenix answered.

The Capital

We jes' want to show her,
some of the town.
How through givin' and carin,'
joy and peace can be found.

"Well, you all have the right guide for that," Sally said, referring to Aristophenix. Then lowering her voice she confided, "That is, if the poetry doesn't just drive you crazy."

Denise smiled back. She was already beginning to like this Sally camel-person.

"What was that?" Aristophenix asked.

"Not a thing, sugar." She grinned. "Not a thing." Then, changing the subject, she asked, "Say, Listro Q, is that a new coat?"

Listro Q practically beamed with pleasure (which is a hard thing to do when you're trying to be cool). "Like it, do you?" he asked.

"Honey pie," she said, reaching out and stroking its fine texture with one of her hands, "it's simply divine."

Again, Denise had to smile. She couldn't say for certain, but it looked like Listro Q's chest actually grew an inch or two larger.

"Say," Sally asked, again changing the subject, "did you all know that today's my birthday?"

"Why, that's right," Aristophenix said. "Happy birthday!"

The others offered similar congratulations.

"Thank you so much," she said, giving a little curtsy. "And since it is my birthday . . ." She turned to Aristophenix. "Would you mind too terribly if I gave you this here pocket watch? It was my great granddaddy's." She pulled out an ornate gold watch from the pocket of her skirt and handed it to him.

"Woo-wee!" Aristophenix exclaimed as he took it into his hands. "Sure you don't mind, ol' girl? It's a beaut."

"It'd be my greatest pleasure."

And it was. Denise could tell by the look on Sally's face that she really enjoyed giving the gift away.

The others crowded around Aristophenix for a better look. After the appropriate *oohs* and *aahs*, Sally finally spoke. "Listen, there's plenty more people down thataway," she said pointing toward the village, "who're just dying to meet your lovely friend here. And since I've got myself a lot more gifts to be passing out, if you all don't mind, I'll just be moving along."

Again she reached out to hug Denise. "It was nice meeting you, girl, and if you're ever in my neck of the woods, be sure to stop by, you hear?"

Denise smiled. "Thanks."

They finished the hug, more fiercely than the last, and Sally was off. "Bye-bye, now," she called as she drifted up the path as graceful as any four-legged camel with two arms can drift. The others called out their good-byes as Denise gingerly tested her side for any broken ribs.

Samson spoke again, and for the first time Denise thought she understood. Well, not all of it. Well, okay, so it was only a general impression, but a general impression was better than no impression. Maybe she was finally starting to get the hang of this place. Or maybe it was because her personality and Samson's seemed to be so similar.

In any case, Aristophenix was the one to respond. "Sorry 'bout that, partner, I'd almost forgot." Turning to Denise he explained,

> **To help Samson graduate**
> **was the purpose of this trip.**
> **He must show you Fayrah,**
> **so from his diploma he don't get, uh, gypped.**

The Capital

This time, the entire group groaned. Usually they were able to endure his poetry, but once in a while he fired off a zinger that was just too painful to ignore. Still, Aristophenix paid little attention as he turned and led them down the knoll toward the village.

Denise threw a look over her shoulder and asked, "Shouldn't Nathan be here by now?"

"Worry, don't you," Listro Q assured her. "As long as stays he in Fayrah, perfectly safe is he."

Denise nodded. Although still a little reluctant, she turned to join the group as they headed down the hill toward the city.

"How much farther is it? Do we have to walk so fast? Aren't we there yet?"

The boy's questions were wearing on Bobok. The only way he could continue was by reminding himself what a delectable catch the Upside Downer would be. But they'd have to hurry. Not only were Bobok's nerves wearing thin, but there was less than two hours of his season remaining in Fayrah. Less than two hours before the Portal sealed itself shut.

"Perhaps if you left that canteen behind," he offered, "it would be easier for you to travel." Ever since he had seen the canteen, Bobok feared it. But he wasn't afraid of the canteen; it was the contents.

"This stupid canteen's not the problem," Nathan complained, rubbing his hip. "It's how fast you're making us go."

"The Portal is just past the courthouse, most favored Thread. But we must circle behind the buildings to avoid the idle chatter of its citizens—lest they contaminate you with their weakness of thought."

"My leg is hurting," Nathan whined. "Besides, you never said it would take this long. Why can't I at least see some people? I still don't know why we have to go so fast."

Bobok continued forward, beginning to wonder if being the most evil and dreaded ruler in seventeen dimensions was really all it was cracked up to be.

Now they were inside the Capital, and Denise was becoming quite the celebrity. It seemed everywhere she went she was surrounded by crowds of excited citizens. The glowing Blood Mountains had signaled everyone that she had entered their kingdom, and now they all wanted to wish her well. Apparently being a member of the Upside-Down Kingdom was quite an honor.

"Ain't this somethin'?" Aristophenix shouted over the crowd.

"I'll say," Denise answered as she reached up to shake claws with a giant twelve-armed crab. "Are they always this happy?"

"Sadness only have we," Listro Q called, "when out-give one another, try we."

Denise broke out laughing. Somehow she wasn't surprised.

"Oh, and girl?" Aristophenix said.

> **If ya' need somethin' else
> to erase all them frowns,
> jes' look over yonder
> with them big baby browns.**

Denise turned. Despite everything she'd seen so far, there was no way she was prepared for this. In front of her stood a magnificent courthouse made of brilliant marble. Every stone was perfectly cut and gleaming white. In fact it was so white, it almost hurt her eyes. Almost, but not quite.

High atop the building, past a hundred glimmering steps, twelve elegant pillars, and windows of what could only be pure

The Capital

crystal, stood the town clock. Its ruby hands glowed and shimmered in the bright morning sun as they pointed to half past ten.

Aristophenix spoke again,

> **This here's our courthouse,**
> **where our money never laxes.**
> **Fact, it's at this very spot,**
> **that the government pays us taxes.**

Next, Listro Q pointed to another building equally as beautiful and grand. "Library, here is it," he said. "All Fayrahnians keep we records do."

"Records?" Denise asked.

Listro Q nodded. "Every deed good of our, every kindness of action, written and recorded in the books."

Denise nodded. It sounded like the library was where they kept records of every Fayrahnian's good deed.

Suddenly Samson began to chatter. This time the tone of his voice said something was wrong.

Denise turned and looked down the street. She had never seen anything like it. It was as if the entire kingdom came to an end. But not all at once. Gradually, the sky drew lower and lower, while turning darker and darker. Slowly, the ground rose higher and higher, its grass and flowers turning sickly brown then black. And on the sides, the trees and bushes crowded closer and closer together, as they also withered and appeared to die. It was as if they were inside a giant pop bottle that narrowed into a tiny little neck. A tunnel. A tunnel where everything, every plant, every color, where all of life seemed to shrivel and die.

"There!" Listro Q pointed. "The Portal!"

Denise squinted. At the far end of the tunnel was a small

round opening where wind and sand swirled fiercely—a small round portal that opened slightly and closed slightly, opened slightly and closed slightly . . . as if it were alive.

But it wasn't the Portal that caught Denise's breath. It was who was heading for the Portal. "Nathan!" she cried. "Mr. Hornsberry!" Then she saw a third creature who seemed to be leading them.

"Bobok!" Aristophenix cried.

She spun to Aristophenix for an explanation. For the first time since they'd met, she saw fear in his eyes. "What's going on?" she demanded. "Where's Nathan going? Who's that with him?" Her voice grew high and shrill, the way it always did when she was scared. "Aristophenix! Aristophenix, answer me!"

The furry creature tried to sound relaxed and controlled. But he was as bad an actor as he was a poet.

> **This ain't a time to worry**
> **or appear too terribly glum.**
> **But that fella hurryin' Nathan,**
> **well, he ain't a Fayrahnian chum.**

"Bobok! You called him Bobok! Is he a bad guy?" Denise cried.

Aristophenix swallowed and tried to look the other way. But Denise wasn't backing down. She wouldn't quit until she had an answer. Finally he looked back at her.

> **Nathan's heading to Keygarp,**
> **that's where he will be.**
> **From Bobok's Kingdom of Winter,**
> **he may never get free.**

Denise's jaw dropped open and she stared helplessly. This is exactly what she had feared since the beginning. Something awful was going to happen. She had known it all along. She spun back to the Portal . . . just in time to see Nathan and Mr. Hornsberry crawl through the opening and disappear.

"Nathan!" she shouted. "Nathan, come back! Mr. Hornsberry!" But she was too late. They were gone.

Listro Q broke from the group and started toward the tunnel. "To go Keygarp!" He shouted. "Come, let's!"

But Aristophenix called out, bringing him to a stop.

> **Hold on ta yer horses,**
> **I don't think that we should.**
> **If we go on inside there,**
> **it might be for good!**

"What are you talking about?" Denise demanded. She could feel her ears burning with anger. "We've got to get Nathan. He's in danger—you said so yourself!"

> **The Portal seals at noon,**
> **that only gives ninety minutes,**
> **to get in and get out,**
> **or become permanent tenants.**

It was Samson's turn to argue with Aristophenix . . . and he did, long and loud, until Denise could take no more. "What's going on?" she demanded. "What's he saying?"

Listro Q's translation was quick and simple. "Help needs Nathan. Help must we."

Denise turned back to Aristophenix. It was obvious that he felt sick over what had happened and that he took full responsibility. It was also obvious that he knew something had to be done.

Once again Samson began to chatter.

And once again Listro Q agreed. "Choice no other have we."

Aristophenix stared at the Portal another long moment. Then, swallowing back his fears, he took a deep breath and started toward it.

Denise and the others followed. Of course Aristophenix tried his best to stay in the lead, because as everyone knows, leaders are supposed to lead. Unfortunately, his roly-poly body hadn't quite gotten the message. So with every step he waddled, he fell just a little farther behind.

> **Slow down on them tootsies;**
> **c'mon, let me pass.**
> **I know there's a hurry,**
> **but I'm runnin' outta . . .**

No one heard his final word. It was lost forever as they entered the howling tunnel of wind and sand.

CHAPTER SEVEN

The Portal

The first thing Nathan noticed as he stepped through the blowing Portal of wind and sand was the heat. But it wasn't the wet and sticky kind. This was hot and dry—the type that pounds your head and makes your eyes ache from its brightness.

The second thing Nathan noticed were the insects. Thousands of them. They were four or five inches long with pincer jaws. And each and every one of them had a single thing in common. They were racing straight for him!

"Bobok!" he cried. "What do we do? What do we do?"

"Close your mouth!" Bobok shouted.

"What?"

"Close your mouth! They smell the moisture from your breath and want it."

"But—"

"Close your mouth and breathe through your nose—*now*!"

Nathan would have argued, but he barely had time to obey. He closed his mouth and just in time. The insects reached his legs— hundreds of them—and quickly scampered inside his pants around his ankles and calves. Instinctively he tried to kick and slap them aside, but there were just too many. As soon as he knocked off one, a dozen more appeared in its place.

"Stop it!" Bobok shouted. "Let them have their way. It will only last a moment."

By now the creepy things were swarming around his knees in their desperate search for water. As they raced back and forth, his skin tickled and itched. But Nathan wasn't moving. Not anymore. He was too frightened. Forget being frightened. He was *petrified*!

"That tickling you feel is only their tongues," Bobok assured him. "They're licking the sweat off your skin—don't worry."

But Nathan was worrying, big time. He looked down and his eyes widened. He could no longer see his legs. He could see their shape okay, but his blue jeans were no longer blue. They were a mass of black and brown insects. Not only were they racing inside his pants but they were outside as well—thousands of hairy legs, fluttering wings, and hard-shelled bodies swarming as they slowly worked their way up his thighs.

Nathan tried his best not to scream. He clamped his jaw shut, he bit his tongue, he did everything he could do. But it was just too much. He had to open his mouth! He had to cry out! He had to—

"CHILDREN!"

All movement around his legs ceased.

"CHILDREN, COME DOWN FROM THAT HANDSOME UPSIDE DOWNER THIS VERY INSTANT!" The voice screeched with power—like steel dragged across concrete.

In seconds, Nathan's legs were completely free of the insects. Completely!

They pulled back into a teeming, swarming wall several feet high and several yards long. A teeming, swarming wall that had obeyed the voice, but remained close . . . just in case the voice changed its mind.

"You'll have to excuse their eagerness." The voice was much softer now, almost comforting. "It's been a long time since we've had the privilege of such a wonderfully handsome visitor with so much . . . moisture."

Nathan finally took his eyes from the quivering mound of

The Portal

bugs to see who was speaking. She sat on a throne and was gorgeous, heart-stopping—a woman more beautiful than any he had ever seen. She had soft blonde hair that fell to her delicate shoulders, a kind smiling mouth, and the most incredible violet blue eyes. Nathan liked her instantly.

"Who is she?" he whispered to Bobok.

"Don't be deceived by her looks," Bobok warned. "The Illusionist is as crafty with her disguises as she is with her words."

Pretending not to hear, the lady motioned to the wall of bugs. "You'll have to excuse the little ones. You Upside Downers consist of so much moisture that sometimes they forget themselves."

"She's trying to scare you," Bobok said. "Don't fall for it."

But Nathan wasn't frightened of her. How could he be? The lady was so lovely and kind.

The pile of droning bugs, however, was another matter. He glanced at Mr. Hornsberry to see how he was taking it. The dog didn't seem to mind them at all. And why should he? As a stuffed animal he was made up of cotton batting and cloth—not much moisture there. But the lady . . . for some reason he seemed very suspicious of the lady. And when she looked at him, a faint growl escaped from his throat.

But instead of anger or concern, the lady broke into a gentle smile. "My, what a beautiful dog," she said. "Isn't he the most perfect thing?"

Immediately Mr. Hornsberry's tail thumped in the sand. So much for suspicions.

"Come here, boy," she called as she knelt down and patted her lap. "Come on."

He gave one of his throat-clearing coughs and nervously answered, "I don't wish to be too terribly rude at this juncture of our relationship, but it's probably best if I remain here with Master Nathan."

"Oh, and he talks," she said with a delighted grin. "Isn't he just the most clever thing?" Turning to Nathan, she added, "What a lucky young man you are to have such a friend."

Mr. Hornsberry's entire body gave a shudder of delight.

The lady rose from her throne and addressed Bobok. "My dearest and most trusted friend, you promised two specimens. I see only one and he's a boy—though an incredibly intelligent and handsome boy to be sure. But where, dear heart, is the girl you promised?"

"She will be coming soon," Bobok purred. "Trust me."

The lady smiled warmly before turning her focus back upon Nathan. "And why have you left her behind?"

Nathan swallowed hard and looked at the wall of thirsty insects. For the first time in his life, he wasn't sure if talking was such a great idea. The lady saved him the effort.

"Of course." She smiled in understanding. "It is because a young man of your special genius and chosen talents would only be held back by someone of her mediocre skills."

Nathan's eyes widened in surprise.

"I am correct, aren't I?" she asked sweetly.

What could he say? When she was right, she was right. And isn't that exactly what Bobok had said—that he was special, a Chosen Thread? Nathan gave a modest shrug and finally spoke, "Yeah, I guess."

Immediately the buzzing from the wall of insects grew louder in agitation . . . or was it anticipation? Maybe it was both. In any case, Nathan knew they definitely smelled the water from his breath and were hoping to race back for seconds on drinks.

The Portal

However, the Illusionist gave a single wave of her hand and they immediately fell silent.

She continued, her voice filled with sympathy and understanding, "It must be very difficult for a good-looking young man such as yourself, with so many gifts and talents, to deal with such an *average* person as the girl."

Nathan looked at her carefully to see if she was mocking him. But there was no irony in her eyes . . . only the kindest, most sincere look.

He gave another shrug. "Sometimes."

The Illusionist nodded in compassion as she approached and gently rested her hand upon his shoulder. "Poor boy," she consoled. "I understand."

"Dear lady," Bobok quietly warned, "remember our agreement. The boy is coming with *me*."

"Of course, my esteemed friend. Though I must say I would give half my kingdom for someone with such looks and great intelligence to stay and keep *me* company."

Nathan looked up at her. He couldn't help smiling. She returned it and gave his shoulder the slightest squeeze. It wasn't much, just enough to say, *Even though we've only met, we really understand each other, don't we?*

"Dear lady . . ." Bobok's warning grew more stern.

"Oh, kindest Bobok, you needn't worry." Directing her gaze back to Nathan she continued, "All I am saying is that it must be terribly frustrating to be as great as he is and have to deal with commoners like that girl." She gave him another little squeeze.

"Oh, it's not so bad," Nathan said. "I mean, she can be pretty stupid sometimes, and, well, yeah, sometimes she's a real pain, but—"

❏

"Ahhhh . . ." Denise doubled over in agony. She had never felt

63

anything like it. They had just entered the tunnel and had started for the Portal when a searing pain ripped through her mind.

"Wrong's what?" Listro Q was immediately at her side. He shouted over the wind, "Happened what?"

"My head!" she gasped.

But it wasn't her head. This was no headache she was experiencing. It was deeper . . . *much* deeper.

Then the pain suddenly left—disappearing as quickly as it appeared. Denise lifted her eyes, dumbfounded.

"Okay, are you?" Listro Q yelled. Even above the roaring wind and whistling sand, it was possible to hear the concern in his voice.

"Yeah," she said, slowly rising. "What was that?"

Aristophenix joined them. "What's wrong?" he yelled over the wind.

"I don't know," Denise shouted. "But I'm okay now."

"You sure?"

She gave him a nod.

"Good!" Aristophenix pointed ahead. "'Cause we've not much time!"

Denise followed his finger to the Portal. Through all the blasting wind and sand, it was still possible to see it widen and contract, widen and contract—as if it were breathing. And each time it contracted, the opening shrunk just a little bit more. She understood Aristophenix perfectly. It soon would close.

The pain that had filled her head was completely gone. Now there was only the stinging sand. It bit her face and arms, and it made her eyes water so badly that she could barely keep them open.

But she had no right to complain. Samson was the one who really had it rough. The little guy fluttered his wings for all he was

The Portal

worth and still barely held his ground against the wind. He chattered loudly for everyone to hurry and continue moving. They did.

Then it hit Denise again—only worse. This time the pain was so intense that it knocked her to the ground. She grabbed her head. But it wasn't just her head. It was as if all of her mind, her body, her personality—everything about her had been hit. Hit hard. In fact, the pain was so violent that all she could do was lie there and gasp.

"Is it what?" Listro Q cried as he dropped to her side. "Is it what?"

But Denise couldn't answer. She was too busy trying to breathe.

"Nathan!" Aristophenix shouted. "It's Nathan!"

Once again the pain shut off. But this time it left Denise much weaker . . . and confused. "What . . ." She panted, trying to catch her breath, trying to make sense out of it. "What's going on?"

Suddenly Listro Q understood. "Speaking bad about you, is Nathan. His words hurting you."

"It's because he's an Upside Downer," Aristophenix explained.

**Your words can cut
and force others to bleed.
'Cause they're spoken from mouths,
which have been Imager-Breathed.**

"You mean . . ." Denise coughed as they helped her to her feet. "Nathan is doing all this to me with his mouth? This is all happening because of what he's saying?"

Listro Q and Aristophenix nodded.

"Great authority have Upside Downers. Powerful very, blessing or curse their words."

"Okay, fine," she called. "He wants a fight, I'll give him a fight."

Taking a deep breath, she shouted at the top of her lungs, "Nathan Hutton O'Brien, you are the world's most—"

"No!" Suddenly both creatures covered her mouth with their hands, or paws, or whatever you'd call them.

Listro Q looked stern. "Spoken *never*," he said, "harsh words in Fayrah, *never*."

Samson chattered again. By now he was several feet behind them and losing ground rapidly.

Aristophenix nodded and yelled,

> **Oh, Sammy boy's a-fadin';**
> **let's get on with the show.**
> **He can't last much longer,**
> **so come on, let's move it! Let's go!**

Listro Q nodded and shouted, "Form a wall, quickly let's!"

"Good idea, partner."

With that, both creatures raced back to Samson. Turning to face the wind, they formed a type of shield with their bodies to protect their little friend. Samson ducked behind them and was able to avoid most of the wind as they struggled back toward Denise. Once they arrived, they linked arms with her and continued forward.

The Portal was only twenty feet ahead, but with the blasting wind and sand it could have been miles. And the opening was growing smaller; there was no doubt about it. It wasn't shrinking quickly, but like the hour hand of a clock, it continued to make progress—slowly but surely.

And still they pressed on . . . heads lowered and shoulders bent to protect their faces from the biting sand. Two steps forward, a slip and one step back. One step forward, a stumble, another step back. Yet, somehow, they made progress. Like the Portal itself, they may have been slow, but they were determined.

It happened a third time—a blow to Denise stronger than the other two combined.

She wasn't sure, but she thought she might have lost consciousness. One moment, she felt the impossible pain. The next moment, Aristophenix and Listro Q were on the ground beside her shouting, "Denny, can you hear us? Denny!"

When she was finally able to speak, she groaned, "Thanks, Nate, that was a beaut."

"Stand, can you?" Listro Q shouted. "Denny! Stand can you?"

Denise wanted to break out laughing. And she would have if she'd had the strength. "You gotta be kidding," she moaned. "Stand? I can barely breathe . . ."

CHAPTER EIGHT

A Hasty Exit

"Well, that's enough talk about that silly old girl," the Illusionist continued in her soothing, silky voice. "But please, you've been so modest. Tell me more about yourself. What a wonderful life you must live, being a Chosen Thread, traveling in and out of dimensions as you do."

Once again, Nathan looked into her understanding eyes. Somewhere deep inside, he felt a stirring—that same rush of excitement that came every time he manipulated a situation to his advantage. It was a wonderful mixture of victory and self-importance. And the best thing was that he didn't even have to work to earn that feeling. Not here. It just came naturally. All he had to do was listen to her compliments and look into those eyes.

Bobok rolled back and forth as if growing nervous. "Dear lady, we would love to talk, but there is much to be done."

Ignoring him, the Illusionist looked directly at Nathan. "Oh, please stay," she begged. "Your visit has given me such courage and strength—just to be in the presence of someone like yourself. Please, don't leave—not yet."

What could Nathan do? That little rush of excitement he'd felt growing inside was now a raging current. How could he say no to someone who admired him so much? How could he refuse to allow her to adore and worship him? Without taking his eyes from hers, he spoke to Bobok, "We can stay a couple more minutes, can't we?"

"I think not, Chosen Thread. There is much to give you in my kingdom, and it will take much time for you to acquire all of its possessions."

"But," the Illusionist protested, "if he stays here with me, he will be loved and admired for his greatness."

"Admiration is important, dear lady. But what of taking? Acquiring possessions is of great importance to a thread of this stature. Am I not mistaken, Chosen One?"

Nathan faltered a moment. It was true. The little blue guy had a point. Being admired was one thing. But having whatever he wanted whenever he wanted it, well now, that was quite another. Still, why couldn't he have both? Again he spoke to Bobok, "But if I'm so great and everything, then why can't I be, you know, adored *and* have all the things?"

"Precisely," the Illusionist agreed. "In my kingdom, you would not only have our worship and adoration, which you so richly deserve, but you would share in all our possessions as well."

"*Share?*" Bobok's voice sharpened. "Such a thread doesn't *share!*"

"A poor choice of words." The Illusionist quickly backtracked. "I did not mean *share*, I, too, meant *possess*. He would *possess* all that I have."

Bobok broke out laughing. "And what a lucky creature he would be. Imagine, possessing all of this sand, all of these insects. To think, Chosen Thread, someday this could all be yours."

For a moment, the spell had broken. Nathan was able to turn from the Illusionist's eyes and look at the grinning Bobok. It was a grin Nathan couldn't help returning. After all, it was true. What did this woman have to offer but bugs and sand? Sure, he'd be loved and adored—treated like a king. But a king of what? A king of sand dunes and insects? "I'm afraid Bobok's got a point," he said as he turned to the woman. "I mean, you really don't—"

But that was as far as he got. For as soon as their eyes met, he came to a stop. He wasn't sure if what he saw was inside her eyes, or if it was a reflection upon their surface . . . or if he was even looking into her eyes at all.

Whatever the case, the barren desert had suddenly exploded with life. Everywhere he looked, there were marvelous castles of crystal, sprawling pathways of gold, and lovely parks and gardens filled with flowers. But what impressed Nathan the most were the people. Thousands of beautiful, perfect people—waving, smiling, and applauding. More importantly, they were all waving, smiling, and applauding for him!

"You were saying?" the Illusionist softly whispered. Now she was standing beside him. It was odd; one moment he was looking into her eyes and the next moment they were standing together gazing over the beautiful city and its thousands of citizens.

"Where—where did they all come from?" Nathan asked, breathless with emotion. "They're . . . beautiful."

"Their beauty is only a reflection of yours," she assured him. "Where they came from is of no importance. The fact that each loves and adores you—that is all that matters."

"Who loves you and adores you?" Mr. Hornsberry asked as he looked about nervously. "Master Nathan, I fail to see to whom she is making reference."

"Gracious lady," Bobok sternly warned. "We agreed. Your reflections are most unwelcome!"

"This is *his* illusion, not mine. This is what *he* wants to see."

Bobok turned back to Nathan, speaking louder to get his attention. "Chosen Thread? The canteen you have about your waist, the water."

A Hasty Exit

But Nathan barely heard. He was too mesmerized by the thousands of adoring people calling out to him—beautiful people begging him to come closer so they could admire him, so they could reach out and touch him. How could he refuse? He started toward them. And to his amazement, he discovered that his hip no longer hurt. He didn't even have his limp!

"Master Nathan," Mr. Hornsberry shouted. "What are you doing—where are you going?"

"Those are my people . . . my fans."

"What people? What fans? Master Nathan, you're proceeding directly toward that multitude of insects!"

Nathan had no idea what Hornsberry was talking about. All he saw were the fans.

"Chosen Thread!" Bobok called.

"Leave him be," the lady warned. "If this is the reality he wishes, let him live it!"

Closer and closer Nathan approached the excited, teaming crowd—every one of them desperate for his attention, for his presence, for his slightest touch.

"Chosen Thread!" Bobok shouted. "Your canteen—your water!"

Nathan could barely hear him. The cheering fans were just too loud. He was only a few feet away now. Just a couple more steps and he would be in the center of their loving, adoring arms.

"Master Nathan!" Mr. Hornsberry cried. "Master Nathan!"

Bobok rolled toward him, shouting over the noise. "Chosen Thread! Chosen Thread, aren't you thirsty? Does not this hot, dry sand make your throat ache for water?" Now he was beside Nathan, then under his feet, nearly tripping him in an effort to get his attention. "Chosen Thread, how about a drink of water! It is so hot. I'm so thirsty—aren't you? How about some cool, refreshing water?"

Nathan glanced down at the creature and smiled. *Poor little guy,* he thought. *He's obviously feeling left out. Probably jealous. But why's he making such a big deal about taking a drink?*

"Just open your canteen! Just one sip!" Bobok shouted. "Just one little sip!"

Nathan shrugged. The little guy had obviously been helpful. If he wanted a drink so badly, there was no reason he couldn't have it. And he was right, it was awfully hot. It probably wouldn't hurt to take a few gulps himself. So, partially for Bobok, partially for himself, Nathan reached for his canteen and opened the lid.

That was all it took.

Immediately the adoring fans began screaming. But they weren't screaming in adoration . . . they were screaming in horror. They began pushing and shoving each other—not to get closer to Nathan, but to get *away*! They were shoving and shouting and screaming to get *away* from him!

"Bobok, what's going on?" Nathan cried. "Bobok!"

"Stop it!" the lady screamed from behind them. "Stop it now!"

"Pour it on the ground!" Bobok yelled. "Pour the water on the ground!"

"But they're leaving!" Nathan cried. His lifelong dream was dissolving before his eyes. "Why are they leaving?"

By now the crowd was trampling over one another in their desperate attempt to flee.

"Stop it!" the lady screeched.

"Pour the water on the ground!"

Mr. Hornsberry began running in tight little circles of frustration, shouting, "Do what he says! Do what he says!"

"Bobok, I don't understand!"

"Pour the water on the ground!"

A Hasty Exit

"Do what he says! Do what he says!"

"But—"

"NOW!" Bobok shouted.

Mr. Hornsberry could stand no more. Suddenly the chubby fellow leaped into the air, opened his mouth, and chomped down on Nathan's wrist. Hard.

"OW!" Nathan cried as he grabbed his hand, dropping the canteen to the sand.

And then it started. . . .

As the water of letters and words poured from the canteen onto the ground, they started to sizzle and pop. Like some sort of powerful acid, they began eating into the sand, turning it into a clear, dark liquid.

"Get back!" Bobok shouted as he rolled away from the rapidly growing puddle. "Get back! Get back!"

Nathan and Mr. Hornsberry didn't need a second invitation. They leaped backwards and watched as the liquid letters ate into the sand, making a bigger and bigger pool—a bubbling pool that began to swirl as it liquefied everything it touched.

But it was not just the pool that held Nathan's attention. It was the reflection in that pool. Now at last he was able to see the illusion for what it was. There were no castles, no golden paths, no flowery hills—just sand. And there was definitely no crowd of adoring fans. As Nathan looked at their reflection he saw them for what they were—a mound of teaming insects, a mound that he had nearly walked into and that had nearly devoured him! But now the mound was collapsing as the insects tried in vain to scurry away from the widening pool.

"My children!" the lady cried. "My precious children!"

But it did no good. The growing, spiraling pool continued to eat away at her kingdom. Maybe *eat away* wasn't the right phrase. Maybe *dissolve* would be better. In any case, Nathan watched with horror and fascination as the pool continued to grow and suck in the sand . . . the insects . . . everything that it touched.

"*Run!*" Bobok shouted over the roar of melting elements.

"What's happening?"

"It's the water from the stream—it is destroying the Kingdom of Seerlo! Run!"

Nathan started to run, but he wasn't quick enough. The very sand under his feet was being sucked into the pool, faster and faster. He began losing more ground than he was taking.

"Jump!" Bobok yelled. "Jump and run! Jump and run!"

Nathan understood and started leaping. So did Hornsberry. And with each leap dozens of yards of sand rushed by under their feet. Up ahead he saw a dark blue forest. But instead of racing toward it, it was racing toward him! As more and more of the desert was sucked into the pool, the forest quickly approached!

"You'll pay for this!" the lady screamed over the wind and roar of melting elements. "I swear, you'll pay!"

Nathan looked up and was amazed at what he saw. It was the lady's voice, all right, but it was no longer the lady—or at least as he'd seen her. This time the Illusionist appeared entirely different . . . a scaled and war-scarred body, with huge cloven hoofs. She had black leathery wings that were now unfurled and flapping—wings that lifted her high above the swirling whirlpool of what had once been her kingdom.

"Hurry, Chosen Thread!" Bobok shouted as he rolled ahead of them, spinning so fast he was merely a blue blur. "Hurry!"

CHAPTER NINE

Keygarp

Although the Portal was only a few feet away, Denise wasn't sure she could make it. She'd already used most of her strength just to stand. After the beating she'd taken from Nathan, she doubted she was strong enough to fight any more sand and wind. Still, there was something about Samson's, Listro Q's, and Aristophenix's encouragement . . . and their love—the way they stayed right at her side, helping her. Somehow it gave her strength, and enabled her to stagger the last remaining steps toward the opening.

The Portal continued to expand and shrink, expand and shrink, as it grew smaller and smaller. Once they arrived, Samson was the first to enter, then Listro Q, then Aristophenix. Now it was Denise's turn. It was more than a little spooky, stepping through something that seemed half alive. But taking a deep breath and closing her eyes, she crawled through the opening and entered. . . .

**Now hold on to yer horses,
I don't mean to harp.
But what happened to Seerlo?
This here looks like Keygarp.**

The group stood inside some sort of frozen forest. But instead of leaves, each of the twisted and gnarled tree branches was covered in layers of frost and ice. That was Denise's first impression of the place—frost and ice. And the color blue. It seemed everything was blue. From the midnight blue of the tree trunks and boulders, to the lighter shades of blue for the snow, to the clear blue layers of crystalline frost that coated everything. There was no yellow, no orange, no red . . . only blue. It was both eerie and beautiful.

Denise gave a shudder and pulled up her collar against the cold. Listro Q and Aristophenix did the same with their clothes—though Listro Q made an extra effort to ensure his tuxedo was free of any sand or debris.

"You there—Upside Downer!" The voice was harsh and raspy, like the cawing of a crow.

Denise looked up. "What on earth?"

The others followed her gaze. Through the twisted branches of the forest they saw a creature with cloven hoofs and covered in scales. It circled high over their heads, its black wings stark against the cold blue sky.

"I have not forgotten!" it cried. "You have been promised to me. I have not forgotten!" And then, with two mighty thrusts of its wings, the creature sailed off.

Denise gave another shudder. Turning to the group, she croaked, "Who . . . who was that?"

No one had an answer. But, even now, Denise suspected it would not be the last time they met.

"Look!" Listro Q pointed in the distance. "Castle Bobok's!"

Denise turned to see a craggy set of towers that seemed to defy gravity as they leaned and loomed in all directions.

"Alrightee then," Aristophenix took a deep breath for courage.

> **To help Nathan, let's move,**
> **since that's what we chose.**
> **'Cause there ain't much time left**
> **'fore the Portal is closed.**

Keygarp

He started toward the castle and the others joined him. Denise hesitated, took her own breath for courage and followed.

◙

The doors slithered open with a harsh hiss. Like everything else in Bobok's castle, they were made of smooth, cold steel. And like everything else in Keygarp, they were covered with a thin coating of frost that sparkled in deep blue light.

Nathan had learned the hard way not to touch the walls or doors or anything else in the castle. Actually, the touching wasn't the problem. It was the letting go that got a bit painful. The steel was so cold that once you touched it, it was impossible to let go without leaving a layer of skin forever frozen to its surface.

They had barely left the forest and entered the castle before Mr. Hornsberry sidled up close to Nathan. "I do hope I'm not speaking with impropriety," the dog whispered between chattering teeth, "but I don't fancy this place, Master Nathan—I don't fancy it one bit."

Nathan had to admit he wasn't too fond of it either. In fact, as they moved from room to room, he wasn't sure if he was shivering because of the cold or because of fear. Maybe it was both.

The next room they entered was like all the others—a large, cavernous hall that seemed to have no purpose except to echo their footsteps. And, like every other room, the walkway was lined on both sides with little orbs that rolled onto their faces as Bobok, Nathan, and Mr. Hornsberry passed. Each frosty-blue ball wore a helmet and had a small sword strapped to its side. But, since they had no arms, Nathan figured the swords were more for show than anything else. And, like Bobok, each had a set of sunken little eyes.

Nathan couldn't help thinking how everyone in the castle looked exactly the same. They reminded him of one of those assembly lines where the same part is stamped over and over again. That's what they were—stamped, carbon copies. Carbon copies of Bobok. Only these creatures had no personality. They were just stamped carbon copies that moved in perfect synchronization with no life or feeling.

Oh, and there was one other thing Nathan noticed . . . a hum. He'd heard it when they'd first entered the castle. And now, with every footstep, it seemed to grow louder.

They approached a pair of doors that towered a dozen feet over their heads. Bobok rolled to a stop and turned to Nathan. "You'll like this," he purred, his voice as smooth as when they'd first met. "You'll like this a lot."

He turned back to the doors and they whisked open. A blast of cold air hit Nathan so hard that he had to close his eyes. And when he opened them . . . well, let's just say he wished he hadn't.

The three of them approached the edge of a platform a hundred feet high. Before them floated dozens of strange creatures—some as thin as pencils, some as round as beach balls, some with three eyes and one head, others with three heads and one eye. Amazing. If you could imagine the strangest imaginables imaginable, and then imagine them just a little bit stranger . . . well, at least you'd be getting close.

"What—what is this place?" Nathan stuttered.

"Welcome to my menagerie!" Bobok beamed.

Nathan continued to stare. The creatures rotated inside a giant cone that stretched a hundred feet above them and a hundred feet below . . . a cone of energy that crackled and sparked every time someone or something bumped against its side. Each of the creatures looked like they had been in a thousand fights. They were scarred and beaten and battered. Their strange, exotic clothing was torn into a million shreds.

Keygarp

But what frightened Nathan even more was how everyone seemed to be in some sort of trance. Although their eyes were open, it was as if they couldn't see. When they drifted into one another, they automatically began to fight and scratch. Sometimes it was over a shred of clothing or a scrap of floating food or even the remains of a shattered toy. But it was always done in slow motion—as if the creatures were being controlled. As if they couldn't help themselves.

Finally there was the matter of the hum. Nathan no longer wondered about its source. It came from here. And it really wasn't a hum. It was a groan. Dozens of groans. Long, slow, mournful groans coming from the throats of these strange creatures caught within the energy field.

"Who . . . who are they?"

"Oh, just different beings I've collected from different kingdoms," Bobok purred. "But they all have one thing in common—at least they do now." He chuckled. "Each is possessed with greed—pure, unadulterated greed."

Nathan stepped back as two creatures passed so close he could have reached out and touched them. Like the others, they kept fighting, slowly and mechanically.

Mr. Hornsberry let out a long, low growl.

Bobok paid little attention and continued. "Once they're in that energy field, they are under my power. They're doomed to scratch and claw, to take and steal for eternity. Great sport, wouldn't you agree?"

Nathan continued to stare.

"Particularly for those who never give but want only to possess."

Nathan tried to respond but he had no voice.

"However," Bobok purred as he turned toward Nathan, "in all my years I've never had an Upside Downer in there . . ."

Nathan swallowed hard. Slowly he turned to look at Bobok. He wished he hadn't.

The blue orb was grinning his grin again. A grin that said his wishes were about to be fulfilled.

CHAPTER TEN

The Menagerie

At first Denise didn't notice the guards at the drawbridge. She just thought they were a couple of larger-than-normal snowballs. Granted, they were bluer than the rest of the snow, and granted, they just happened to be wearing helmets and swords, but, hey, it had been a long day. She was entitled to make a few minor mistakes.

Unfortunately, these two guards were anything but minor.

"Who goes there?" Guard One shouted.

The group slowed to a stop and looked at Aristophenix. The pudgy bear cleared his throat and announced,

> **We're from the land of Fayrah,**
> **and though meeting you is a treat,**
> **we're looking for a boy**
> **and an orb who needs feet.**

Listro Q rolled his eyes at him.

"Hey, it's the best I can do under pressure," Aristophenix whispered.

The two guards paid little attention. Instead, Guard One approached a tree stump next to Listro Q and effortlessly rolled up its side. Now he stood on its top, about waist high. "Fayrahnians?" he asked. His voice sounded mechanical and brittle—like some old-fashioned record.

"Right are you," Listro Q answered, obviously trying to remain cool. Though it's hard to remain cool when you're sweating from fear.

"Nice coat," the guard said as he rolled closer and rubbed against Listro Q's tuxedo jacket.

"Uh, er, thanks."

"Give me," the guard demanded.

Listro Q hesitated. It was obviously one of his favorite possessions. No way would he give it up. At least that's what Denise thought. But then the most amazing thing happened. Without a word, Listro Q reached down and started unbuttoning it.

"What are you doing?" Denise asked. "You love that coat!"

"Shhh," Aristophenix whispered.

Everyone watched as Listro Q took off his coat, then slowly laid it on the stump beside the little blue ball.

But instead of showing gratitude or even giving a "thanks," the guard immediately demanded more. "Nice shirt. Me want shirt, too."

Listro Q frowned and tried to reason. "Cold, freezing is it," he said.

"Me want shirt!" the guard insisted. "Me want shirt! Me want shirt!"

With a reluctant sigh, Listro Q reached down and started unbuttoning his shirt.

"This is ridiculous," Denise muttered as she pushed up her sleeves and started for the little orb.

"Denny," Aristophenix warned.

"There're only two of them and four of us," she said.

"It's not the Fayrahnian way."

"I don't care whose way it is," she argued. "They're just a couple twerpy little ice balls, and if you're not men enough to stop them, then I'll—"

But that was as far as she got. Because when she turned back to the guard she discovered the little "ice ball" had grown five to six times in size. Now it was as tall as she was!

"Whoa!" she cried in surprise. "What happened?"

The Menagerie

"Your hate," Listro Q said, as he finished unbuttoning his shirt and handed it to the guard, "fed him did it."

"My hate did this?" Denise asked, marveling.

The blue ball grinned.

"But . . ." Denise turned in frustration to Aristophenix. "You guys just can't stand around and give them whatever they want."

Samson chattered off a response. Aristophenix nodded and translated.

> Give what they want,
> do what they say.
> That's our code of love;
> that's the Fayrahnian way.

"But that's not fair!" Denise could feel the tops of her ears burn again, a sure sign of her anger. The same anger that made her the terror of every bully in the schoolyard. The same anger that would attack any foe, no matter what their size, even five-foot-five, round, blue ones!

But when she turned back to the guard, he was no longer five foot five. Now he was ten foot ten!

"Augh!" she screamed. She threw a look over at Listro Q, who only shrugged as if to say, *I told you so.*

Before she could do any more damage, Aristophenix reached into his vest pocket, pulled out the gold watch that Sally the camel creature had given him, and took a look at the time.

> My, oh my,
> well, what do you know?
> We'd stay for a chat,
> but it's time we must go.

Now Guard Two rolled forward. "Nice watch."

But he had a little competition. For even though the first guard had Listro Q's shirt and coat, he was still greedy enough to try for the watch as well. "Yeah," Guard One said, "*very* nice."

Why, this little thing?
Shucks, it's all rusty and old.
Though I guess that's not rust,
since it's made of solid—

But no one heard Aristophenix's last word as he "accidentally" dropped the watch to the ground. Before he could complete his poem, the two blue balls rolled for it.

Now it's true, Guard Two was many times smaller than Guard One, but as they fought and shouted and struggled for the watch, he began growing in size.

"Quick! Go let's!" Listro Q shouted as he scooped up his shirt and coat.

"But—" Denise protested.

"Hurry!"

She obeyed and followed as they raced across the drawbridge toward the castle. Suddenly there was a violent explosion behind them, followed by another. Denise spun around. The giant blue orbs were nowhere in sight. Instead, a light blue snow had started to fall.

"What happened?" she shouted.

"Snow!" Listro pointed.

"I see the snow, but where'd those guys go?"

"Here," Listro Q said, again pointing to the snow.

"You mean . . . this is them?" Denise couldn't help grinning in satisfaction. "This snow is them?"

The Menagerie

"Correct are you."

"They blew themselves up?"

"Critical mass," Listro Q nodded. "Their hatred blew up them."

"All right!" Denise laughed. "Well, I guess you guys really do know what you're doing, don't you?"

No one answered. Instead, all three stood there giving the weakest smiles she'd ever seen. Suddenly she wasn't quite as confident. "You did know that was going to happen . . . right?"

Again, they smiled.

"Oh, brother," she sighed. For if there's one thing she'd learned, it was that Fayrahnians couldn't lie. They could smile all they wanted, but they could not lie. "You mean to tell me you just guessed this would happen? You just winged it?"

Once again the trio smiled.

"Oh, brother," she muttered again as she turned and headed into the castle. "Oh, brother . . ."

Aristophenix, Listro Q, and Samson looked at one another, shrugged, and followed her inside.

▣

"If you think I'm going in there," Nathan said, backing toward the door, "you're crazy!"

"You are a chosen thread," Bobok insisted as he rolled toward him. "To take and possess without giving, to look out only for yourself—that is your dream."

Nathan continued backing away. "Yeah, but . . ."

"This is what you've lived for, what you've always wanted."

It was Mr. Hornsberry's turn to speak. The hair on his back was sticking straight up, and although he remained polite, there was no missing his determination. "Excuse me, but if you persist in rolling any closer, I am afraid I shall have to take a bite out of your head."

Bobok threw him a glance and chuckled lightly. "This is my kingdom, oh cloth stuffed with cotton. You will do as *I* say." Bobok continued moving toward them.

"I have given you sufficient warning," Mr. Hornsberry said, sounding as bold as any English bulldog could sound—although he would have been a little more convincing if he hadn't been shaking or crowding so close to Nathan's legs.

Bobok continued toward them.

"Please . . . ," Nathan stuttered. "Maybe we can talk, you know, work something out."

Bobok continued.

"It is quite obvious, Master Nathan, that the creature wishes no further dialogue." Mr. Hornsberry turned to Bobok. "Am I correct in this matter?"

Bobok said nothing, but continued.

"Very well," Mr. Hornsberry said, "have it your way—though please remember, I did give you sufficient warning." With that the dog leaned back on his haunches and with a fierce growl sprang directly at Bobok.

But the ruler was prepared. He fired off a blast of icy cold breath that hit the animal dead center. And there, in midair, Mr. Hornsberry froze. He didn't even fall to the ground. He just hung there, suspended.

"Mr. Hornsberry!" Nathan cried, racing to him. He reached out and touched him. The dog felt as cold and stiff as a chunk of ice. Spinning around to Bobok, he demanded, "What have you done to him?"

"It makes no difference," Bobok purred. "In a matter of seconds, you will no longer care."

Nathan threw a cautious glance back at the menagerie.

The Menagerie

Another pair of fighting creatures drifted by, lost forever in their mindless trance of scratching and clawing, grabbing and owning, taking and possessing. "I . . . I don't want to go in there!"

"All of your life, Chosen Thread, you have been planting the seed of greed. Now it is only fair that you enjoy its harvest."

"But . . . that's not what I wanted!"

"It is precisely what you wanted. To live in a world where all you do is take."

"Yes, but—well, not like that." He threw a terrified look at the menagerie. "I didn't mean this. I didn't . . . what I meant was—"

Bobok started to laugh. It was cold and frightening.

Nathan's fear turned to panic. He had to make a break for it—past Bobok and out the door. But Bobok sensed his thoughts and signaled the guards. Their speed was amazing—blue blurs that raced to the doorway—hundreds of them—until Nathan's escape was entirely blocked.

Turning back to the menagerie, Nathan shouted, "I won't go in there! You can't make me!"

Bobok said nothing. Instead he simply nodded to the guards. Like a synchronized machine, the little balls rolled out across the platform and slowly closed in. Nathan had to back up—closer to the edge of the ramp, closer and closer to the menagerie.

"Please . . . ," he begged. "Don't do this . . . I beg you . . . *please*."

Bobok only smiled.

Nathan glanced over his shoulder. There was only a few feet of platform left. Just a few feet before he'd fall into the cone of energy. He turned back to Bobok. "*Please* . . ."

The orbs continued forward.

He reached the edge of the platform. He began fighting to keep his balance.

The guards pressed ahead.

"*Please . . .*"

"Enjoy yourself," Bobok grinned. "I know I will."

And then it happened. Nathan's foot slipped. He tried his best to hang on, but it did no good. With a chilling scream, he tumbled and fell.

The energy cone crackled and surged with power as if Nathan had somehow fed it, as if his spoiled selfishness had given it energy—an energy that it would feed upon for many epochs to come.

CHAPTER ELEVEN

The Rescue

"Hurry!" Denise shouted as she ran ahead of the group into a giant hall of the castle. "This place is huge! There must be a hundred rooms to check."

"Shut and seals the Portal . . ." Listro Q looked at his watch. "In thirty-eight minutes!"

"Thirty-eight minutes?" she cried. "Can we find him in time?"

"And free Nathan," Listro Q added, "and return to Portal and escape through Portal all of us. Doubtful, is it."

"But . . . we've got to try!" Denise insisted.

Samson began to chatter.

"Yes, I hear it," Aristophenix answered.

"Hear what?" Denise demanded.

"Low hum," Listro Q said, cocking his head to hear better.

Denise strained to listen. She heard it, too.

Samson chattered some more.

"Are you sure, ol' boy?" Aristophenix asked.

Samson gave a terse answer.

"What?" Denise demanded. "What's he saying?"

Aristophenix turned and explained,

> From his studies, he has knowledge,
> that to me seems far-fetched,
> 'bout a room full of moaning,
> where Bobok's prisoners are kept.

"That could be their moaning!" Denise cried. "If Nathan's his prisoner, all we have to do is follow the hum!"

The theory seemed as reasonable as anything else in this place. Again everyone grew silent, straining to hear what direction the sound was coming from.

"Over there!" Denise said, pointing at a door to the left. She raced toward it. "Come on!"

The door hissed open and she dashed in, followed by the others.

Now, tracking a hum wasn't as easy as Denise had thought. Especially in a castle with a maze of twisting hallways—hallways that often came to a dead end for no apparent reason. More than once the group zigged when they should have zagged, and headed down a few stairways when they should have headed up. But after plenty of frustration and confusion, they somehow made it to the front of a huge, towering door—a door that slowly crept open as they approached.

Denise quickly entered, then slowed to a stop. She had never seen anything like it. Apparently, neither had the others. They were on the ground floor, at the base of some sort of energy cone. It stretched up and out, high above their heads. In here the discordant groans were deafening. They came from zombielike creatures that circled and floated by—each slowly fighting and scratching for the slightest scrap of food, clothes, or toys.

It took some searching, but Denise finally spotted him. "Nathan!"

On the far side of the energy field, several feet from the floor, he was floating. Like the others he seemed to be in some sort of trance. His sweater was already gone and he was slowly and mechanically fighting a strange triangular creature for what was left of his shirt.

"Nathan!" Aristophenix shouted. "Nathan, ol' buddy!"

The Rescue

The others joined in. "Nathan, can you hear us? Nathan! Nathan!"

But Nathan did not hear. Not a word.

"Well, hello there," a voice called from above. Denise tilted back her head to see an ice-blue orb on a platform several stories above them. "Welcome to my little party."

"Bobok," Aristophenix whispered with a shudder.

Denise looked at him, then at Samson and Listro Q. All three seemed equally as frightened. But there was little time to waste on fear. She turned back to Nathan. He was drifting toward them. If she jumped high enough she might be able to reach him and drag him down. She crouched, preparing to leap into the energy field.

"No!" Listro Q shouted, grabbing her arm. "Energy field, touch don't you!"

Denise turned to argue but was stopped cold by the look in his eyes. For whatever reason, Listro Q was deadly serious. All right, fine, she wouldn't jump in. But there was nothing to stop her from getting as close to Nathan as possible and waking him by shouting. She broke free from Listro Q and moved to within inches of the field. "Nathan!" she yelled. "Nathan, can you hear me?"

He continued drifting around, closer and closer, until they were nearly face-to-face.

"Nathan? *Nathan!*"

But Nathan gave no sign of recognition. Instead, he continued the slow mechanical fight over his shirt.

The voice above their heads broke into cold laughter. "Call all you want, my dear, he'll never hear you. He's mine now—doing what he's always wanted."

Denise looked up at the creature. "I don't know what you are," she shouted, "but I want him back, and I want him now!"

He gave another ominous laugh.

"Listen, you little ice ball!" she yelled. "If I ever get my hands on you, you're going to be—"

Suddenly the energy field flashed and sparkled brighter. Suddenly the groaning and moaning grew louder. And suddenly Listro Q's hand was upon Denise's shoulder.

"What did I do?" she protested. "I was just—"

"Hate of yours." Listro Q motioned toward the energy field. "The more have you hate, the more has it energy—like the outside guards."

"But . . . ," Denise sputtered in frustration. "We have to do something!" She turned to the furry bear. "Aristophenix! What do we do?"

Aristophenix stared at her, blinking.

"Come on, you're supposed to be the leader! What do we do now?"

But he had no answer. There were no longer any pithy poems, no blustery proverbs. The only answer he had was in his eyes. And in those eyes she saw the look of hopelessness.

"Aristophenix?" she cried.

"I'm . . . sorry," he said.

Not believing her ears, she turned to his partners. "Samson! Listro Q?"

Both stared hard at the ground.

"I don't believe this!" she yelled. "I don't—"

Suddenly Samson interrupted. He spoke only a few words before the other two joined in.

"Yes!" Listro Q shouted.

"Of course!" Aristophenix cried.

The Rescue

"What?" Denise demanded.

"Bloodstone, still have you?" Listro Q asked excitedly.

"What stone?"

**The stone from the mountains,
with which you signaled us first.
It's a bit of a long shot,
but it might break the curse.**

"You mean Nathan's birthday gift—from your Blood Mountains?"

"Have it, still you?" Listro Q repeated.

"I think . . ." She began digging into her pockets. "Yeah, here it is."

"Wonderful!" Listro Q exclaimed as she handed it to him.

Samson chattered again.

"Hope so, let's," Listro Q answered as he carefully aimed the slightly longer portion of the stone in Nathan's direction.

"What's going on?" Denise demanded. She seemed to be asking that a lot lately, and didn't seem to be getting any answers.

Once Listro Q had the stone carefully positioned in his hands, he gave a nod and Aristophenix spoke to Samson.

**Okay, ol' boy,
let's give it a shot.
It's all aimed and ready;
let's see what you got.**

Samson swooped down to the stone in Listro Q's hands. Hovering just a few inches above it, he began to buzz his wings harder and faster. And the harder he buzzed, the brighter the blue light in his tail glowed. Denise had always noticed it flickering when he spoke, but now it glowed brighter than ever. In fact, it was so bright that the light began to bounce and reflect inside the Bloodstone until the rock itself started to glow.

"More, lots need," Listro Q urged.

Samson bore down harder. Louder and louder his wings buzzed. Brighter and brighter his tail glowed.

"Hurry!" Aristophenix shouted. "We haven't much time."

Samson continued to work until finally, to Denise's amazement, a single beam of intense red light began extending from the stone.

"Attaboy, partner!" Aristophenix cheered. "Keep it up!"

High above, Bobok laughed maliciously. "Surely, you are not serious?"

No one bothered to answer.

Denise watched with fascination as Listro Q continued to carefully aim the pointed section of the Bloodstone toward Nathan. Slowly the red beam cut its way through the energy field toward the floating boy.

"That's it," Aristophenix cried, "keep her a-comin'! Keep her a-comin'!"

The beam inched its way forward.

"Futile," Bobok mocked them. "Your efforts are futile."

And still the beam continued forward until it was just a few feet from Nathan's face. Then it began to sputter.

"More," Listro Q shouted. "Need we more!"

"He's giving it all he's got," Aristophenix cried.

As the beam continued to sputter it also slowed until its progress came to a stop altogether. It could push no farther ahead. It was as if it had hit a wall—a wall with Nathan just a few feet on the other side.

The Rescue

Bobok's laugh grew louder. "Fools . . . I warned you. Utter fools."

The little bug bore down even harder—buzzing louder, trying to glow brighter. But it did no good.

"Reach him, can't we!" Listro Q shouted. "More, Samson!"

"It's no good!" Aristophenix called. "That's all he's got!"

Denise watched helplessly. She wasn't sure what the red beam could do, but she knew it was important for it to reach Nathan. Important, and by the look of Samson's exhaustion, impossible. Then suddenly, an idea struck her: if she could increase the power of evil by hating and being mean, then maybe, just maybe she could increase the power of good by loving and being kind. It was a long shot, she knew that, but it appeared to be the only shot they had.

"Attaboy," she called to Samson. "Hang in there, fella, you're doing great!"

For a second Samson hesitated, shocked to hear Denise compliment anybody about anything.

"Keep it up, little guy! Come on, you can do it!"

But as she spoke, his determination seemed to grow. He bore down harder and his tail actually grew brighter. Not a lot, mind you, but right now every bit helped.

"That's it," she cheered. "Samson, you're doing it!"

His buzz grew louder, his light grew brighter. And soon the rock was growing brighter. The beam resumed its progress, slowly moving toward Nathan.

"Attaboy," Denise encouraged. "Way to go, Samson!"

The beam continued, inching closer and closer to Nathan— until at last it struck him squarely on the face.

"What are you doing?" Bobok shouted from above.

Life came back into Nathan's eyes. He gave his head a shake and looked around, trying to get his bearings.

"Nathan!" Denise shouted. "Nathan, over here!"

He turned and spotted her. He started to move, to try and free himself from the energy field, but he couldn't. His mind had been cleared, but he didn't have the strength to move his body. "Denny!" he called. "Denny, help me!"

"Nathan . . . listen to me! Listen very carefully!" It was Aristophenix. "We haven't much time. You have to break this power."

Again Nathan struggled against the energy field, but it was just too strong. He couldn't break free.

"You have to stop fightin'," Aristophenix shouted. "You have to stop fightin' them creatures in there and start showin' them love!"

"You're crazy!" Nathan cried. "It's impossible! Not in here— I can't!"

"Yes, you can!" Aristophenix shouted back. "With the power of that light on you, you can do anything!"

"You don't understand! They'll tear me to pieces! I *gotta* fight!"

The light started to sputter.

"Much, too," Listro Q cried to Aristophenix. "Can't last, Samson!"

Aristophenix nodded and shouted to Nathan more urgently. "You gotta show some love . . . trust me! Stop fightin' and show them love!"

But even as they spoke, the triangular creature Nathan had been fighting took advantage of his distraction. With sharp jagged claws he ripped off another piece of Nathan's shirt, deeply cutting into his back.

"Augh!" Nathan screamed in agony. "See what happens?"

"Let him have it!" Aristophenix shouted.

"What?"

The Rescue

"Let him have your shirt! All of it!"

"I can't!" Nathan gasped. "You don't understand, I can't!"

Samson was growing weaker by the second. The beam from the Bloodstone started to flicker.

Spotting it, Denise resumed her encouragements. "You're doing good, Sammy. . . . You're doing real good."

But the truth was, he wasn't doing good. Not anymore. The truth was, he was nearly exhausted.

Aristophenix continued calling to Nathan. "You can give it to him! Give that shirt to him! You gotta!"

"On come!" Listro Q shouted. "Hurry!"

"I . . . I . . ." Nathan's voice grew weaker. Not only weaker but flatter—sounding more and more like the dull monotone voices of the outside guards.

"Too bad," Bobok laughed. "Your plans have failed. They will always fail in my kingdom."

And then, at last it happened. Samson collapsed. He fell to the floor, panting, barely able to catch his breath. The light from his tail had gone out. The red beam from the Bloodstone vanished.

"*Nathan!*" Denise screamed.

But it was too late. Nathan had fallen back into the power of the menagerie. He was back in its trance.

CHAPTER TWELVE

A Second Chance

"Samson! You okay, buddy?" Aristophenix dropped to his knees to help the little bug.

Denise quickly joined them as Samson gasped and tried to gulp in as much air as possible. "Is he going to be all right?" she asked.

Aristophenix hesitated a moment before nodding. "He's young," he said, "but like you, he's stubborn."

Denise threw Aristophenix a look. But it wasn't an insult. In fact, it almost sounded like a compliment.

"Easy there, fella," Aristophenix urged as Samson struggled to get up. "You've been workin' too hard. Easy, little guy."

But Samson would have none of the sympathy. In a matter of seconds, he was back on his feet—all six of them. After a couple false starts, he was able to flutter his wings fast enough to slowly rise off the floor. Once again he was airborne—although his buzzing sounded much weaker than before.

Denise watched with awe and wonder. She could feel herself getting caught up in his determination. Once again she was back on her own feet. And, once again, she was cheering him on. "Attaboy, Sammy! You can do it!"

The encouragement helped. With every positive word she spoke Samson grew stronger.

Nathan had drifted completely around the menagerie and was floating back toward them. This time the beam from the Bloodstone wouldn't have to travel so far; it wouldn't need as much energy from Samson.

A Second Chance

Without a word the little bug took his position over the stone in Listro Q's hand. He started buzzing his wings and glowing his tail. There was no missing the stress and strain he was under. But he wasn't about to give up—not this time.

Neither was Denise. She stepped up closer to the hovering bug and quietly whispered into his ear—telling him how impressed she was, what a big heart he had, how much she appreciated and, yes, even admired him for what he was doing.

And that made all the difference in the world. . . .

A new surge of brightness shown from Samson's tail. The Bloodstone started to glow. Finally the shaft of red light burst forth, and in moments it struck Nathan squarely upon the face. Once again the boy regained consciousness. By now he and his fighting partner, the triangle creature, were just a few yards away.

Spotting Aristophenix, Nathan again pleaded, "Please, you gotta help me!"

"There's nothin' more we can do!" Aristophenix shouted. "Only you can choose to break his control—and there isn't much time!"

"But—"

"You've got the power!" Aristophenix insisted. "Just use it!"

"Come on, Nathan!" Denise called. "You can do it!"

For the briefest second, Nathan appeared surprised at her encouragement. Come to think of it, so did Denise.

"Watch it!" Aristophenix shouted. He pointed to a pair of fighting prisoners who started drifting between Nathan and the beam.

Listro Q dropped to his knees, shooting the beam underneath the fighters so they would not interrupt its flow of power.

"Nathan," Denise cried. "You can do it! I know you can! Just stop fighting and give that thing your shirt!"

Again Nathan looked at her. She wasn't sure if it was the

99

power from the beam or from her words—maybe it was both. But somehow, somewhere Nathan found the strength to slowly lower his arms and begin unbuttoning what was left of his shirt. Of course the triangle creature went in for the kill. And, of course, his sharp, jagged claws dug deep into Nathan's chest.

"Augh!" Nathan screamed. But this time he would not give up. This time he continued unbuttoning his shirt.

"You are fools," Bobok mocked from his platform. "Fools!"

The beam started to weaken. Though Nathan was closer, Samson didn't have the strength he had in the beginning. Still, between seeing Nathan's efforts and hearing Denise's words, the little bug pressed on.

At last, Nathan unbuttoned the final button. He started pulling his arms out of the shredded sleeves.

"Attaboy!" Denise shouted. "You can do it, Nathan, you can do it!"

"Fools!" Bobok shouted. "Fools!"

Samson's light began to sputter.

"Hurry, lad," Aristophenix shouted. "Hurry!"

The shirt was off. But that was only half the battle. Now Nathan had to fight the menagerie's power. Now he actually had to reach out and show love to the creature. He had to actually give him his shirt.

"Enough!" Bobok shouted. He started rolling back and forth across his platform. "Chosen Thread, this is what you wanted. Nowhere in any dimension will you enjoy so much taking!"

Beads of sweat sprang to Nathan's forehead as he fought and struggled. If he could just overcome the menagerie's control—if he could just utilize the red beam's power and reach out to offer the shirt to his enemy . . .

He started drifting away again.

Samson worked harder, but the blue light of his tail grew

A Second Chance

weaker. The beam from the Bloodstone became more and more faint. Soon it was almost invisible. Almost, but not quite.

"Give it up!" Bobok shouted. "Give it up!"

"Come on, Nathan!" Denise called. "You can do it—you can do it!"

And then, ever so slowly, Nathan started reaching out his arms—arms that held the prized shirt.

"Come on, Nathan, I know you can do it!"

"Stop that!" Bobok shouted. "Stop that at once!"

Slowly, inch by torturous inch, Nathan made progress until, at last, his arms were fully extended to his enemy.

With a vicious growl, the triangle creature snatched the shirt from his hands, and suddenly . . . suddenly, the entire energy field crackled. Then, to everyone's astonishment, it began losing power.

"My menagerie!" Bobok cried. "Look what you've done! Look what you've done!"

Like a giant machine the menagerie slowly wound down until it came to a grinding halt. The groans of the prisoners faded as each regained consciousness and gently floated to the ground. Many shook their heads in confusion, trying to remember where they were or what had happened. And, as the realization sank in, they began to murmur among themselves—a murmur that grew into shouts of joy!

"Nathan!" Denise cried as she raced to him. The others ran onto the floor right behind her. Before she realized it, she had thrown her arms around him in a giant hug. "I knew you could do it!" she shouted. "I knew you could!"

Nathan couldn't return the hug. He could only stand there, dumbfounded at the love he was receiving from her. Still, there was no missing the glint of moisture in his eyes. And there was no missing the thick hoarseness in his voice when he finally spoke. It wasn't much of a sentence—only one word. But a word Nathan hadn't used in years.

"Thanks . . . ," he said. Unsuccessfully he tried to swallow back the lump in his throat. "Thank you . . ."

By now the other three had managed to work their way into the embrace. In fact the entire floor was full of creatures hugging, celebrating, and congratulating one another.

But it didn't last long.

Bobok's voice echoed through the room. "After them!"

Immediately hundreds of little blue orbs that had surrounded Bobok began leaping from his platform onto the floor of the menagerie. Many of them were hurt by the fall or crushed by fellow orbs landing on top of them. But those who survived had one goal—to recapture the prisoners before they escaped!

Panic swept the crowd. "What do we do?" they shouted. "We're lost! He'll capture us again!"

Then, just before everything turned to chaos, Aristophenix raised his cane high above his head and shouted,

> **Onward to the Portal,**
> **there's not a second to waste.**
> **It soon will be sealed;**
> **let's move, let's go, make haste!**

With his cane still above his head, the roly-poly bear waddled forward and the crowd followed. They raced out of the menagerie and through the rooms of the castle until they reached the drawbridge and crossed it. Then it was into the bare, frozen forest of Keygarp. Yet, for some reason, none of Bobok's little blue guards followed.

"Where are they?" Denise shouted to Aristophenix.

Panting hard, the bear tried to answer, "Look at your feet!"

Denise looked down and saw that the hard ice and snow were turning to slush. "It's melting!" she yelled in surprise.

A Second Chance

"The whole kingdom—inside and out," Aristophenix shouted. "The guards can't roll in slush—not like packed snow."

They continued through the forest. Trees dripped with water as the ice on them melted. Icicles gave way, clattering and shattering as they hit the ground. Then, at last, Listro Q spotted it.

"There!" he shouted, pointing in the distance. "There is it!"

Denise looked and saw the Portal. But even from their distance, she could see the breathing opening was much smaller . . . and growing smaller by the second!

"Hurry!" Aristophenix called to the group. "It's almost sealed!"

Panic filled the crowd as they pushed forward.

"Samson!" Denise cried. She looked every direction but couldn't find him. "Where's Samson?"

"Here," Listro Q said. He held out his pocket—a pocket that glowed and pulsed as Samson looked up and chattered away at her.

Denise grinned.

So did Listro Q.

When they finally arrived at the windy Portal, Aristophenix took a position beside the opening and began directing the crowd through it. Listro Q joined him. For many of the creatures it was going to be a tight squeeze, but with Aristophenix and Listro Q's help, they were able to make it. "Be careful of those antenna . . . tuck in all of your legs, ma'am . . . watch your heads, sir . . ."

"Mr. Hornsberry!" Nathan shouted.

Denise turned to see the bulldog racing through the forest as fast as his stubby little legs could carry him. "Master Nathan, wait for me, wait for me!"

"You're unfrozen!" Nathan cried.

"An accurate observation," the dog said as he arrived, then leaped into Nathan's arms, practically knocking him over.

"Everything in the kingdom is thawing."

But their joy was short-lived. A noise filled the forest. It was an ominous chant—half living, half machine.

"LUMM-KUMM, LUMM-KUMM, LUMM-KUMM."

The ground itself vibrated with the sound. . . .

"LUMM-KUMM, LUMM-KUMM, LUMM-KUMM."

Denise watched as Bobok's army emerged from the woods— hundreds of them—rolling in perfect precision. Although they were slowed by the slush, their progress was steady and constant—like a slow-moving machine—a machine that would not be stopped. . . .

"LUMM-KUMM, LUMM-KUMM, LUMM-KUMM."

Terror filled the crowd. Desperately they began to push and shove at one another, doing anything they could to be next through the Portal.

"Please, everybody!" Aristophenix shouted. "Wait your turn!"

But his request was met with only more screams and shoving as the army of blue orbs continued their approach.

"LUMM-KUMM, LUMM-KUMM, LUMM-KUMM."

"Them all through," Listro Q called, "get can't we!"

"We gotta try!" Aristophenix shouted over the noise.

"LUMM-KUMM, LUMM-KUMM, LUMM-KUMM."

Suddenly there was the sound of a whinnying horse. All heads snapped back toward the forest to see Bobok appear on a midnight-blue steed. He quickly trotted past his troops to take command.

The prisoners' terror grew to near riot. Everyone knew Bobok's power—his persuasive logic—his overwhelming evil. And now he and his cold blue orbs were less than fifty yards away—fifty yards and closing in!

"No good is it!" Listro Q shouted to Aristophenix.

Denise turned to the crowd. Listro Q was right. It was hope-

A Second Chance

less. There were still twenty or thirty creatures to help through the Portal. They couldn't possibly get them through in time. Either the Portal would seal or Bobok's army would move in—or both! What could they do? Where could they turn?

Samson began to chatter.

"That's what?" Listro Q asked, opening his pocket and allowing Samson to fly out.

Samson repeated himself.

Immediately Aristophenix shook his head. "No, no, that's too risky."

"What?" Nathan shouted.

Denise joined in. "What's he saying?"

But Aristophenix wasn't answering. He was still debating with Samson. "No, I haven't got a better idea, but—"

Again Samson chattered.

"Samson . . . ," Listro Q warned.

Whatever Samson was saying, he was not giving up. He kept right on arguing until Aristophenix and Listro Q started running out of excuses.

And still he chattered away.

At last, his two friends exchanged uneasy glances.

"Sure are you, Sammy?" Listro Q asked. "This something is of sure are you?"

Samson answered even more impatiently.

Listro Q turned back to Aristophenix. Apparently a decision had to be made. And apparently it could only be made by Aristophenix. The furry creature shifted his weight uneasily.

He looked at the panicky crowd as they screamed and pushed their way to the opening. . . .

He looked at Bobok's army who were much, much closer. . . .

And finally he looked at Samson.

Then, slowly, sadly, he began to nod. "Okay," he said. But by the catch in his voice, Denise could tell it wasn't okay. It wasn't okay at all.

Immediately Listro Q reached into his pocket and pulled out the Bloodstone. He threw it several feet behind them, directly in front of Bobok's approaching army.

Samson followed the stone and once again began hovering over it.

Fear shot through Denise. "Samson!" she shouted. "Samson, what are you doing?" She turned and started for him but Listro Q caught her. "Let me go!" she yelled. "Let me go!"

Listro Q's grip was firm.

"Let me go! He's not that strong!"

"No!" Listro Q said.

"Let me—"

"Stop it!" Listro Q shouted. And it was the intensity of that shout that caused Denise to stop struggling. She looked up into his face as he spoke. "Only way, is it." And then more quietly, "Only way . . ."

Denise blinked, then swallowed. She turned to watch as Samson buzzed his wings furiously over the rock . . . as the army continued its approach. Once again he generated a blue light from his tail. And once again that light started to bounce back and forth inside the Bloodstone until a bright red glow suddenly burst out. But since Listro Q wasn't there to direct it, the light was no longer a beam. Now it formed a huge red circle—a circle whose color the army could not look at—a circle that forced them to stop their advance.

"Aughhh!" Bobok yelled as his horse began prancing and bucking. "Stop that light! Get that bug!"

The army tried to inch their way forward, but they could not approach the light. It was an impenetrable wall of color. A wall

A Second Chance

that protected Samson and the few remaining prisoners as they exited through the Portal.

"Quickly now!" Aristophenix encouraged the group. "Don't look back! Quickly!"

Samson continued hovering over the stone, but his buzz was much weaker. He simply hadn't had the time to recover from his last ordeal.

Cautiously, the army surrounded the wall of color, until they had formed a circle around Samson and the stone.

"Destroy him!" Bobok shouted. "Stop the color! Destroy the bug!"

Yet the army would not, they could not, penetrate the red glowing wall.

Unfortunately, it was a wall that began to shrink as Samson's strength began giving out.

"Come on, Samson!" Denise shouted. "You can do it! You can do it!" But even Denise's words didn't help.

Samson's light grew fainter and fainter. The wall of color shrank smaller and smaller. Relentlessly, Bobok's army closed in tighter and tighter.

"He can't make it!" Nathan cried.

"Quickly," Aristophenix shouted to the last of the prisoners as he ushered them through.

Samson had nearly reached exhaustion. The wall was only a few feet around him now . . . and so were the hundreds of blue orbs.

"Destroy him!" Bobok screamed.

"Nathan!" Aristophenix shouted. "Nathan, you're next!"

Nathan looked up as the last prisoner squeezed through the Portal. There was just the five of them left.

"Now, Nathan!" Aristophenix shouted. He had wedged his way into the opening trying to keep it from closing completely. But his efforts were in vain. Although he was slowing it, it was obviously he could not stop it. "Nathan!"

Looking back at Samson, Nathan was obviously torn.

"There's nothin' you can do for him—not now! Trust me!"

Nathan continued to hesitate.

"Now, or we're *all* doomed!"

Finally, reluctantly, Nathan ducked his head down, and still carrying Mr. Hornsberry in his arms, he quickly squeezed through the Portal.

"Denny!" Aristophenix called. "Denny, you're next!"

But Denise wasn't moving. All she could do was stare at Samson. The poor little critter was near exhaustion. He had less than a foot of light surrounding him. Less than a foot of color to protect him from Bobok and his army.

"Denny!" Aristophenix shouted. "Denny!"

But she would not budge, she refused to budge . . . until Listro Q suddenly picked her up.

"Put me down!" she cried. "Put me down!"

And then it happened. At last Samson's light flickered out.

"Samson!" Denise's heart broke as Bobok's thugs lunged toward her brave little friend. "Samson!"

To spare her the awful sight, Listro Q covered her eyes and pushed her through the opening.

She cried one last time. "*Samson*!" But it did no good. Her voice was lost in the howling wind.

Listro Q followed right behind her. Then Aristophenix—and just in time. For as the pudgy creature unwedged his body from the opening, it slammed shut with a foreboding *boom*.

The Portal was sealed.

CHAPTER THIRTEEN

Home, at Last . . .

Denise and the rest of the group stepped out of the tunnel and into Fayrah. As before, it was a perfect day with perfect weather. But for some reason the colors seemed more vivid than before—glowing reds, bright greens, vibrant yellows. Maybe it was because they'd spent so long seeing nothing but the blue hues of Keygarp. In any case, the colors of Fayrah were so pure and beautiful that for a moment Denise's eyes almost ached with pleasure.

Then there were the citizens—thousands of them. They all come out to greet the newly freed prisoners. It was a time of joy and celebration. Everywhere there was laughter, backslaps, and shouts of delight as long-lost friends and relatives found one another in the crowd.

Denise and Nathan seemed to be the only ones having a difficult time of it. Granted, they tried to smile as they were congratulated and they did their best to look happy. But neither of them was too successful. They had lost a friend—a good friend. And no amount of backslapping or laughter could take that loss away.

"He was . . . *good*," Denise quietly said to Nathan.

Nathan nodded. "Yeah."

Seeing their sadness, Aristophenix cleared his throat and tried his best to encourage them.

> **Don't be so downhearted.**
> **There's no need to stew.**
> **After all, Sammy boy just did**
> **what all Fayrahnians want to do.**

Denise forced a smile. It was almost good hearing Aristophenix use his poetry again. Almost. It would have been better if Samson had been there to complain about it with the rest of them.

"He did what all Fayrahnians want to do?" Nathan repeated. "What do you mean?"

"Same love as Imager," Listro Q quietly explained. "Able to experience same love, was he."

"All he did was die. What good did his dying do?" Nathan challenged.

"So free are you," Listro Q answered. Then, motioning toward the thousands of happy Fayrahnians before them, he continued, "So, too, are others."

Denise wanted to argue, but as she looked around to the crowd of freed prisoners . . . and as she looked at Nathan . . . well, somehow, the argument fell flat. Somehow she suspected that Samson's love *did* do some good. And she suspected something else. She suspected Nathan's speeches about looking out for number one would never again be spoken with the same conviction as before. That didn't mean he wouldn't still be a selfish brat from time to time, but . . . well, something inside Nathan was changing. She could see it. And she didn't mind it. Not in the least.

Finally, glancing up at the courthouse clock, Aristophenix cleared his throat and spoke.

> **Don't mean to be party-poopers,**
> **or make you feel more low.**
> **But your grandpappy'll be a-worryin',**
> **if toward home we don't roll.**

"Home," Denise quietly mused. It seemed like a million miles away. Joshua, Nathan's brother, was probably just finishing

Home, at Last

basketball practice. Grandpa O'Brien was probably back in the shop with the puppy. And her mother—well, her mother would still be at the diner taking orders and clearing tables.

"Got them coordinates, ol' buddy?" Aristophenix asked.

Listro Q gave his standard answer. "Cool."

Aristophenix nodded and turned to the crowd. "Folks!" he called. "Folks, may I have your attention?"

The crowd grew silent and Aristophenix continued,

**Our friends have to leave us;
it's sad, we all know.
But you just can't travel to,
without traveling fro.**

The crowd groaned slightly.

"Push them buttons," Aristophenix whispered to Listro Q. "I'm losin' 'em."

"Cool," Listro Q answered as he gratefully reached for the little Cross-Dimensionalizer.

The crowd began waving and calling out best wishes to Denise, Nathan, and Mr. Hornsberry, which the three returned—until Listro Q set the coordinates and pressed the four buttons.

BEEP!........BOP!........BLEEP!.......BURP!....

Suddenly the group was bathed in intense light. More suddenly, still, they were falling. Again they were surrounded by other lights who were also falling—falling gracefully and smoothly. Each headed toward the bright concentration of light in the middle—the Center.

The thought of heading back there didn't make Denise leap for joy. She remembered all too well what had happened the last time she took this route.

She looked around nervously. As her eyes grew accustomed to the light, she spotted Mr. Hornsberry, Listro Q, and Nathan. But once again this Nathan was the older, more mature Nathan—the one with the shield and the suit of armor. Only this time he didn't have his swords—the ones fashioned out of the canteens and covered with bug blood. Hmm, sometime she'd have to ask him if he knew what that was about.

Right now, though, the Center was coming into clear view. Already she could see the thin layer of fog and beyond that the bright, glowing buildings.

Closer and closer they came as Denise tried to think of a pleasant thought. She wasn't about to go through what she'd been through the last time. No way. She had to fill her head with something good. Anything good.

But she was trying too hard. Nothing came to mind. Maybe a Christmas present here, a compliment there. But they were such short thoughts she knew they wouldn't last—not all the way through the Center. She started to panic. They were nearly there and no thoughts were coming. Desperately, she searched for something . . . anything.

Aristophenix! she called. *Aristophenix, help me!*

Suddenly a pair of hands tenderly covered her eyes. For a moment she struggled, trying to fight them off, to push them away. But they would not move.

And then she smelled it. Aftershave. But not just any aftershave. It was the same aftershave her dad used to wear. It had been years since she'd smelled it. In fact, until now, she had completely forgotten about it.

She had also forgotten how her mother had kept his clothes in

Home, at Last

the closet. How they had remained there for what seemed like years after he left. And how as a little girl, she used to sneak into the closet, stand on her tiptoes, and bury her face into his favorite flannel shirt. She would just stand there pressing her face to it, breathing in the smell of his aftershave . . . and remembering.

That was happening now—the remembering. She could feel her whole body start to relax. Slowly she leaned into what she remembered to be her daddy's arms. And, strangely enough, they were there to support her. Deeper and deeper she relaxed, as she continued to breathe in, as she continued remembering his strength and tenderness.

The light outside the pair of hands grew incredibly bright. Then there was the singing. It was beautiful. Denise wanted to look, but knew she would be too terrified at what she saw. Besides, this was better. Resting in these arms was safe—secure. As long as she stayed there nothing could touch her.

Eventually the light and singing started to fade. And finally the hands were removed. Denise didn't bother to turn and see who they belonged to. She knew no one would be there—not now.

She looked for the Center and was surprised to see that it was above them and not below. They had passed completely through it and had come out the other side. Now she was heading away from it—but not wildly and out of control like the last time. This time everything was smooth and easy.

The light from the Center rapidly faded. Then, the faint outline of walls, ceiling, and a floor appeared around her. At last the sensation came to an end. The group was back inside the Secondhand Shop. Everything was exactly as it had been. There were no surprises.

Well, maybe one . . .

"*Samson!*" Nathan shouted as he spotted the half dragonfly, half ladybug. The little critter was buzzing over the Bloodstone.

"Samson! You're alive!" Denise started running toward him, but she'd only taken a couple steps before she caught herself. It wasn't Samson. Oh, sure, it looked like Samson; it flew and sounded like Samson. But this one's taillight was red. Samson's was blue.

"Congratulations, ol' boy," Aristophenix called out to the bug. "Glad you could join us!"

Denise turned to Aristophenix. "Hold it," she said. "That can't be Samson. He's dead."

"Right is that," Listro Q agreed. "Dead and alive."

Denise frowned and for the first time that she could remember, Aristophenix broke into a big grin!

Suddenly the insect dive-bombed her a couple times, then began buzzing around her head—all the time chattering in delight.

"But . . ." Denise hesitated. "If he's, you know, *dead* . . . how can he . . ."

Aristophenix chuckled.

> **I'm so sorry, Denny**
> **I thought that you knew.**
> **Fayrahnians have to die,**
> **so their lives are renewed.**

Denise was lost. "But his tail, Samson's was blue—this one's . . . this one's *red*."

> **In giving life we find it;**
> **Sammy boy's passed the test.**
> **The red means he's grown up.**
> **A citizen like the rest.**

Home, at Last

"Samson!" she cried. "It is you!" She did her best to throw her arms around him. But hugging a flying bug isn't the easiest thing to do, as Samson zipped in and out of her arms chattering a mile a second.

"What's all that noise out there?" It was Nathan's grandfather. He was in the back room. "Nathan, is that you?"

Aristophenix quickly whispered,

> **We'd better get a-goin',**
> **don't have much time to waste.**
> **We'd love to surprise him with a howdy,**
> **but heart attacks are in such bad taste.**

"Nathan?" Grandpa called again. The lights to the shop snapped on.

Suddenly Denise had a new concern. "Will we ever see you again?" she whispered. She had just lost one good friend and found him; she didn't intend to lose any more.

"Certainly, yes," Listro Q assured her.

"Are you sure?" It was Nathan's turn to sound worried.

> **Just put that stone in the moonlight,**
> **you know the score after that.**
> **Wherever we are or are going,**
> **we'll swing by for a little chat.**

"Good-bye," Denise whispered. She gave Listro Q a hug. Then she turned and hugged Aristophenix, burying her face deep into his fur.

"Good-bye," Nathan said, shaking both of their hands and doing his best imitation of a grown-up . . . until his handshakes also turned into hugs.

Samson gave a chatter.

"And you," Nathan said, his eyes filling with moisture as he looked up at the bug, "I'll never forget you."

Samson answered and Listro Q translated, his own voice thick with emotion, "Nor we, you."

"Nathan?" By now the old man was shuffling up the far aisle toward them. "Nathan, answer me!"

"Quickly!" Aristophenix whispered to Listro Q.

To which Listro Q, with trusty Cross-Dimensionalizer in hand, answered, what else, but, "Cool."

Turning to the children, Aristophenix whispered,

> **Our journey's been nifty;**
> **it's really been swell.**
> **But now we got to be movin',**
> **so bye-bye, ta-ta, fare thee . . .**

> BEEP!........B⁰P!........BᴸEEP!.......BURP!....

In a flash of light, the Fayrahnians were gone.

And just in time.

"Ah, so there you are," Grandpa said as he rounded the corner. "And would you mind tellin' me now, just where you've—"

But the poor man never finished his sentence. Immediately he was attacked by Denise and Nathan, who smothered him with all sorts of hugs. And if that wasn't enough, they both began talking at once, using new words like *Bloodstone, Fayrah, Aristophenix, Listro Q*—

"Hold it, hold it!" Grandpa shouted until they finally came to a stop. "I asked you a simple question. Now if you don't want to be givin' me a simple answer, then—"

"But we are giving you an answer," Nathan insisted. And once again they bombarded him with even stranger words like *Seerlo, Bobok, Keygarp*—

Again Grandpa's hands flew up. "If you don't want to be tellin' me the truth, then—"

"But, Grandpa, we are telling the truth!"

The old man gave them a scowl and repeated, "If you don't want to be tellin' me the truth, then I'll be hearin' nothin' until you do."

Denise and Nathan exchanged glances. By the look of things, the truth wasn't exactly something he was prepared to hear . . . at least for now. Maybe for now it was better to keep their little journey a secret—just between them . . . and all the rest of Fayrah!

Suddenly, a dog began yelping. Denise turned and spotted an adorable black and white puppy scampering down the aisle toward them.

"Ohhh . . . ," she cooed.

Nathan stooped down to pick him up and immediately received a nonstop face washing.

"Whose is he?" Nathan asked, trying to avoid the wet, slippery tongue that seemed to find every part of his face at the same time.

"Why, he's yours, lad. Don't you remember?"

"But . . . but I have a dog." Nathan motioned toward Mr. Hornsberry, who sat on the counter near the Bloodstone. Only now he wasn't giving speeches or sounding stodgy or being pompous. In fact, right now he wasn't even moving. Instead, he remained as stuffed and silent as when he'd first been unwrapped.

"But that's just a toy," Grandpa said. "This one here's real—it's the one you've been saying you wanted."

Nathan looked back down at the puppy and got another face full of wet tongue.

Denise watched. From years of experience, she knew exactly

what Nathan was thinking. Why couldn't he have both dogs? In fact, why couldn't he have as many as he wanted? If he played his cards right, it wouldn't have to stop here, he could get all the puppies he ever dreamed of.

But then Denise saw something else. Nathan was looking over at the Bloodstone. And by the expression on his face, she realized he was thinking other thoughts . . . thoughts of Blood Mountains, of a kingdom of giving, and of a little dragonfly-ladybug with a brand-new taillight.

Suddenly he turned to his Grandfather. "Grandpa, what time is it?"

"A little bit after nine."

"Do you think the Johnson children will still be awake?"

"Why?" Grandpa asked suspiciously. He obviously knew gears were turning inside Nathan's head. He just couldn't figure out which direction.

"Do you remember when they were here earlier—how badly they wanted a puppy?"

"What's on your mind, lad?"

"I was wondering . . . ," Nathan continued. "Would it hurt your feelings if I, you know, gave the Johnsons *this* puppy?"

"Nathan!" Denise didn't mean to scream but she couldn't help it.

"Lad, have you gone daft? I spent nearly every dime on this here fella."

"I know, and he's super—it's just . . ."

Denise looked on. She could tell this type of thinking was brand new to Nathan, and she wasn't surprised that it took a while for him to put it into words.

"It's just . . . well . . . they wanted a puppy so badly and, you know, I really do have one, and . . ."

Home, at Last

"You feeling all right, lad?" Grandpa slipped his hand to the boy's forehead. "No fever . . . no headache?"

Nathan shook his head. "No, I'm fine. Could we, Grandpa? Do you think that would be all right?"

The old man stood there a long moment—first looking at Nathan, then at Denise, then back at Nathan. Then, without a word, he turned and started for the coatrack.

"Where are you going?" Nathan asked.

"After all of these years," Grandpa said, as he threw on his scarf and coat, "do you think I'd be missing out on seeing you actually give something away?"

"All right!" Nathan shouted.

"Yeah!" Denise laughed. "I'd like to see this myself."

Nathan shot her one of his famous glares but it quickly turned into a twinkle as they headed for the door.

Denise grinned back. She was almost beginning to like Nathan . . . almost. At least she didn't feel like punching him in the stomach. The thought struck her as a little strange. But then again the entire evening had been strange.

The tiny bell above the door gave a jingle as the three of them stepped out onto the sidewalk. It had started to snow again. A gentle snow—the type that slowly covers the dirt and grime of the city and gently smooths out its harsh edges.

Grandpa locked the door and they turned to head up the street. But as they passed the shop's window, Denise thought she saw something inside. She couldn't be sure, but it looked like a tiny red flicker near the counter. A tiny red flicker that could only come from a strange and very unusual stone. A tiny red flicker that seemed to say their journeys weren't exactly over . . . not yet.

Not by a long ways . . .

About the Author

Bill Myers is the author of the humorously imaginative *The Incredible Worlds of Wally McDoogle* series. Bill's latest works include the creation of a brand new secret agent series for early readers, *Secret Agent Dingledorf*. He is also the creator and writer of the *McGee & Me*! video series. Bill is a director as well as a writer, and his films have won over forty national and international awards. He has written more than 50 books for kids, teens, and adults. Bill lives with his wife and two daughters in Southern California